SECRETS IN PARADISE

THE ARCHER INN SERIES BOOK TWO

KIMBERLY THOMAS

Secrets in Paradise
The Archer Inn Series
Book Two
By
Kimberly Thomas

CHAPTER ONE

A SOFT WIND BLEW, TUSSLING RINA'S WAVY BROWN HAIR. SHE brushed a few strands out of her eyes and then took a deep breath. The grass had just been cut that morning, and the air was filled with its succulent scent. *He would like it here*, Rina thought as she stared at the gray slab in front of her, Dennis's name etched into the grey stone. Immediately she felt the pang in her chest and wondered if it would ever go away.

Conner reached over and put a hand on his mother's shoulder, offering her a sad smile. "It's hard to believe it's already been six months, huh?"

Rina nodded. It was both hard to believe six months had already gone by and, at the same time, that it had only been six months. It had felt like an eternity to her. Ever since Dennis's heart attack, her sense of time had been skewed. She was lucky if she knew what day of the week it was most times.

She smiled at her youngest son, then leaned over and nudged

his shoulder with hers. It didn't do much since he now towered over her 5'4 frame, but he let out a short laugh anyway. "More like it's hard to believe it's been eighteen years. I must be getting ancient if my oldest boy is getting ready to go off to college."

"Nah, you're not a day over thirty," Conner said with a smirk. His hazel eyes sparkled with humor. He looked so much like his father when they'd met all those years ago. Sometimes, he would walk through the door, and Rina would freeze for a moment, sure it was her husband who had returned and not her youngest son.

Rina's eyes went wide in mock horror. Hand over her heart, she gaped at her son. "Dear God, I hope not! I know I was a rambunctious girl, but not that rambunctious!" Then, she grinned and winked at him. "I'm only thirty when you kids aren't around."

Conner laughed and nodded, returning her grin. He turned and looked over at his father's gravestone, then nodded his head in Rina's direction. "You hear that, Dad? She's sure got some silly notions in her head, doesn't she?"

Rina smacked her son in the shoulder even as she laughed. He'd always had a strange sense of humor, one he had inherited from his father, in fact. Conner had gotten more from his father than just looks. He really was like a miniature version of Dennis. She was just thankful Trevor, her oldest son, took more after her. She wasn't sure she could've handled three jokers running around the house.

Dennis would have been proud of his son, though. He would be a freshman at LSU this fall. Dennis had been looking forward to having two college students and eventually getting to see them both graduate.

"You know, your father and I were your age when we met,"

Rina told her son. He looked over at her and nodded. He'd heard the story at least a dozen times before, but that didn't stop him from sitting and listening patiently. "We'd both just started college in Miami. He was used to city life, but I was a freshman from Islamorada, as green as could be. God, if it wasn't for your father, I'm not sure I would have survived."

Conner laughed and shook his head. He reached over and put his arm around her shoulder, and she rested against him. "Nah, you would have been fine, Mom. You've always been tough and strong. I'm just sorry this had to happen now, with Trevor and I both away at school. I don't like you being alone in the house by yourself."

"Well, you know me. I've always been married to my work. I'll probably be so busy I won't even notice. And heck, having some peace and quiet around the house means I might actually be able to sit down with a book for once. Maybe even take bubble baths at night..." Rina tried to sound positive, but truth be told, she was just as worried as Conner was. She had gotten so used to having a busy, active house. The kids and their friends running around, juggling work and family events, and all sorts of other bits of chaos that had become normal for her.

Plus, she hadn't worked since Dennis had died. She just couldn't bring herself to focus on event planning while she grieved. Truth be told, she wasn't sure she was done grieving yet. But she had to move on sooner or later, didn't she? And like Conner said, soon, she would be alone in their family house, so she would have to figure out something. Otherwise, she probably would go insane.

But she didn't want to think about that right then. That was too depressing to think about. She needed to change the subject unless she wanted to fall back into that black pit that had become all too familiar over the last half a year.

"Just think, soon you'll be off for your first year of college. Aren't you excited?"

Conner gave his mother a handsome grin, then nodded. "Oh, yeah. I can't wait to check out some of the LSU parties. I'm sure there's gonna be a ton of babes there!"

"God, you really are just like your father!" Rina said with a laugh as she shook her head. She had known Dennis for a little while before they had gotten together, and he'd been a major womanizer. When they had actually started dating, she'd been a little surprised when they hadn't broken up after a couple of weeks. But apparently, he had decided to settle down with her, and she had no doubt the same thing would happen to Conner eventually as well.

Trevor already had found his someone. Shannon was a nice girl, and while Trevor constantly reminded Rina they were only just dating, you didn't date someone for two years unless you really liked them. And with how much he would blush whenever Conner would tease him about just that, Rina could see right through Trevor's claims.

"Don't party too hard," Rina reminded her son. "You still had to keep your grades up. Partying is fun and all, but it's not the only part of going away to college."

Conner gave her that lopsided grin again. He brushed his hair out of his eyes, and once again, Rina was hit with a dose of nostalgia, transported back to her own college days when Dennis would look at her like that. "Don't worry, Mom. I can handle partying and keeping my grades up. Just watch, I'll be at the top of my class and scoring with all the hot girls."

"Conner Renner!" Rina chastised, giving her son a mock glare. "There are certain things a mother does not need to hear about, and the girls you 'score' with is one of them! But either way, you better be using protection. I am far too young to be a grandmother!"

Though truth be told, she really wasn't all that young anymore. Forty-four wasn't old, but she certainly wasn't young, either. And now, there she was, a widowed single mother of two young men. Where was she supposed to go from here? She didn't quite like the idea of spending the rest of her life alone, but it wasn't like the dating market was huge for a woman her age.

Besides, she wasn't ready to date yet either. Even though it had been six months since Dennis had died, it was all still so fresh, so raw. Everyone kept saying it would get easier, the pain would hurt less, that time heals everything, but so far, she hadn't seen any evidence of that. If anything, it had just gotten worse. It seemed like every day she would find something new that reminded her of Dennis.

He had been such a major part of her life for so long, and even the smallest things triggered memories. Sometimes they were memories she hadn't thought about in years, but they were no less painful. The nights were the worst, with her lying awake in her bed, painfully aware of the empty spot next to her.

The spot he'd never again lay in. She would never again get to feel his body heat next to her—only smell his scent on his pillow that she refused to wash. Never again get to wake up in the middle of the night because he'd started snoring too loud. It was funny how she even missed the things that used to drive her crazy.

It was all part of her sense of normality, and without it, she wasn't sure how she would ever really be able to move on. Sure, logically, she knew she would eventually form a whole new sense of normal, one without her late husband, but right now, that just seemed like an insurmountable obstacle. One she wasn't sure she wanted to tackle, either.

She didn't want to move on. She wanted to rewind time, to hold him one last time, to never let him go. But that just wasn't possible, no matter how much she wished for it, no matter how much she prayed. She couldn't go back and change the past. All she could do was keep going forward, even if it meant moving at a snail's pace.

It would have been one thing if it'd just been her left behind. Then, it wouldn't have mattered if she'd just lay in bed all day and given up on the world around her. But she had Conner and Trevor to think about. She had lost her husband, but they had lost their father. And while it may not have been as traumatic for them as it would have been if they'd still been kids, she knew it wasn't easy for either of them.

"He would be so proud of you; you know that, right?" Rina whispered to her younger son. She blinked rapidly, trying to stop the tears that threatened to fall at any moment.

Dennis would've been proud of his son—both of his sons. Conner had graduated with grades good enough to get him into his dream school. And while he may not have been at the top of his class, neither of them had expected him to. All they had ever asked from either of their sons was for them to try their absolute best, and they'd both done that.

Conner took a deep breath and then nodded. His body was stiff against hers, and she knew he was fighting back tears as well. He had been trying to be strong for her, to be a rock for her to lean against, but Rina saw right through his act. She had heard him in his bedroom at night, crying softly. She had talked to him a few times, but while he hadn't exactly shut her out, he wanted to deal with things on his own terms, and Rina couldn't argue with that.

"I'm proud of you, too," Rina added, leaning over to kiss him on the cheek. She'd never been prouder of him, in fact. Not only had he managed to finish out high school while grieving, but he'd been there for her whenever she had needed him. It hadn't been fun, having to rely on her youngest son for comfort, but he had never once turned her away. She wouldn't have gotten through the last six months if it hadn't been for him and Trevor.

Rina's phone buzzed and she fished it out of her purse with a sigh. The text was just an automated one, reminding her about her upcoming credit card payment, so she dismissed it without a second thought. What caught her attention, though, was the time. She muttered a curse under her breath as she scrambled to get up off the ground.

"It's almost six," she told Conner when he looked at her with a raised eyebrow. They were supposed to be meeting Trevor and Shannon for dinner at six, which meant they were going to be late. Somehow, they'd let time slip by them, sitting there reminiscing about the past.

But no matter how much she wanted to, she couldn't live in the past. She had to keep moving forward, one step at a time.

CHAPTER TWO

RINA SLUMPED BACK IN THE SOFT LEATHER SEAT. THE BMW had been Conner's sixteenth birthday present, and he had treated it like his baby ever since. Rina and Dennis had both warned him if he wrecked the car, they weren't buying him another one. But he hadn't let it get so much of a scratch in the two years he had been driving it. If anything, it still looked perfectly new, like it had just rolled off the showroom floor.

Rina couldn't have asked for more than that!

When Rina had suggested visiting Dennis's grave for a bit, Conner had insisted on driving. And while Rina was fully prepared and willing to drive the two of them, she did kind of like being chauffeured around. Dennis had always done the driving whenever the two of them had gone out as well, so it was just another way Conner was like his late father.

The two of them really could've been twins—twins with twenty years between the two of them, but twins nonetheless.

They were going to be late for dinner, but Rina had texted Trevor on their way back to the car. Somehow, he didn't seem surprised. That alone should have told Rina just how much she'd changed in the last six months. She would have never allowed herself to be late for anything. She was always at least ten minutes early to any appointment, no matter how minor. Lately, though, she was lucky if she remembered her appointments, which made it a good thing she had stepped back from her business for a couple of months. After all, what good is an event planner who can barely remember the event?

When her phone went off again, Rina nearly jumped out of her skin. She forced her eyes closed and took slow, deep breaths, trying to get her heart rate back down. She was too wound up, too stressed out. But she didn't think anything was going to help that right then, not even a month at the spa. She just needed to get used to her new normal, assuming that was even possible.

But everyone assured her it was. Grief didn't last forever, they told her, even if it sure felt like it would.

Pulling her phone out of her purse, Rina frowned at the screen. It wasn't an automated text message this time. Instead, it was her older sister calling again. Rina stared at the name for a moment and then swiped her finger along the screen, dismissing the call. She had called a little over a week ago, complaining about the family Inn falling apart like Rina was supposed to just drop everything and rush down to the Keys for her.

"She didn't even know Dennis had died," Rina mumbled under her breath as she put her phone away. "Like she's ever cared about anyone other than herself."

She caught Conner, watching her out of the corner of her eye.

When she turned to look at him, he frowned at her. Never good at subtly, it was obvious he had something on his mind. He was just being a good son and trying to keep his mouth shut.

"Just spit it out," Rina said with a sigh. Whatever he was thinking, it was better to face it head-on than letting it boil up and come to a head.

Conner sighed, his hands tightening around the steering wheel. He shifted uncomfortably in the driver's seat for a moment before glancing over at his mother again. "There are two sides to every relationship. They're not one-way streets. You could've reached out to her, you know. Did you even try to let her know Dad had died?"

Rina sighed and closed her eyes again. Sometimes, she hated that her son had grown up to be such a smart and compassionate man. Life had been easier when she hadn't had to worry about her youngest, making her feel bad with his wisdom.

But even though Conner had a point, he didn't quite understand how things were between Rina and her family. He had only ever briefly met her side of the family. And while Conner and Trevor still got along like best friends, the same wasn't true for Rina and her siblings. She had barely spoken to any of them since the day she'd left Islamorada. And ever since her father died two years ago, she'd had even less incentive to talk to any of them.

"My family isn't the same as ours," Rina told him. She had kept her issues away from her kids as much as possible. They didn't need to deal with those headaches. But Conner wasn't a child anymore, and she didn't want to lie to him. "The Archers... We all left the Keys and pretty much never looked back. After our father died, we've basically kept our lives completely separate."

Conner nodded and then shrugged. "Yeah, I get it. But you

can't really blame Aunt Holly for not knowing Dad died if you never reached out and told them, you know?"

God, Rina hated when he was right. She couldn't really be mad at Holly for that. Not that it really mattered in the long run. She still had a whole list of other things she could be mad at her sister about. But just because Holly had gotten a random urge to go back to the Keys and fix up the old family Inn and try to rekindle their family relationships didn't mean Rina had that same urge.

That ship had sailed long ago.

Thankfully, Conner didn't press the issue. When they finally pulled up outside the restaurant, Rina was glad to have something else to focus her mind on. After spending the day at Dennis's grave, sitting around thinking about Holly and the rest of the Archer clan was not something she quite had the mental energy for.

Even though the restaurant was quite busy with the dinner rush, Rina spotted her eldest son almost instantly. Two inches taller than his younger brother, it wasn't easy for Trevor to blend into a crowd, even sitting down. Shannon was sitting next to him, her hair neat and perfect as always, and Rina had the urge to dig in her purse for a brush. After sitting outside for hours in front of the grave, she could only imagine what her hair looked like.

"You look fine," Conner whispered with a smirk. He'd seen right through her, of course, and she flushed with embarrassment.

She was sure he was just being polite. The thin sundress she had chosen this morning no doubt smelled like grass and flowers, but it was too late to go home and change. None of the other patrons even so much as glanced her way either, and for the first time in years, Rina had to remind herself she wasn't on Islamorada anymore. She would never see any of these people again and wouldn't have to worry about gossip spreading like wildfire.

A child's laughter jarred her out of her thoughts and Rina smiled at her son as she nodded. "You're right. I'm just being silly." The scent of fresh tomatoes and basil filled the air, and Rina forced herself to take deep breaths and relax. This was just a simple family dinner, nothing more. It wasn't like she was out with Dennis, trying to impress clients or anything.

No, that was something she wouldn't have to worry about anymore. The days of not being able to leave the house without ensuring every single strand of hair was in place were behind her. For the first time, she really didn't have to be meticulous in her appearance. It was funny, now that she thought about it. She'd gone from worrying about how she looked because of small-town gossip to worrying about it because of small-minded aristocrats.

Trevor stood when they approached the table. His t-shirt hung loose on his lanky body, his faded jeans looking one wrong move from sliding right off his hips. While he may have had a couple of inches on his younger brother, he had none of the muscle Conner possessed. No matter how many times Dennis had tried to get his son into basketball or another sport, Trevor had always been more at home with the chess team.

"How're you holding up?" Trevor asked in a low voice as he stooped to wrap his arms around his mother. Long gone were the days when they'd been the same height. Rina could barely even remember him being smaller than her!

"I'm fine," Rina assured her eldest. She forced a smile onto her face, but the look Trevor gave her told her he saw right through her little act. But, ever the gentleman, he just nodded, kissed her cheek and slid a chair out from the table for her. Rina slid onto the hard wooden seat, smiling at Shannon, who sat directly across from her. "How are you doing, darling? Enjoying your last little bit of freedom before your senior year?"

Shannon beamed and nodded. "Trying to, but the internship has been working me like crazy. It's like they know I'm going back to school in a couple of weeks, so they're determined to milk as much out of me as they can beforehand!"

"That's an unpaid internship in a nutshell! They teach you some of the hands-on parts of the job and work you near to death at the same time!" Rina laughed and thought back to her own internships during college. She had spent more time running supplies from one place to another than she could remember. But it wasn't just the actual work she did that had been valuable—seeing successful event planners in action had been just as important.

She hadn't realized it at the time, but being worked like a slave had prepared her for just how intense event planning was in reality. It wasn't just sitting in an office in front of magazines, picking out the right tablecloths and napkins. It was also wrangling a dozen different people in charge of the various aspects. Cleaning crews, caterers, supplies, etc., all needed to be corralled; otherwise, nothing would ever get done on time.

Kid's birthday parties had some room for error. But a couple's wedding? Or a big bank charity gala? Not a chance. The food showing up late or the decorations being the wrong color could completely ruin the event. And no matter whose fault the issue was, it fell back on the event planner at the end of the day.

And this was why Rina had always ruled her business with an iron fist. There was no room for error, no matter how small the event would be. If they were paying her to plan something, then she was going to do everything in her power to make sure it turned out perfect.

Maybe that was why she and Dennis had worked so well together. He had worked long hours and so had she. Both of them had taken pride in their work and always strived for more. And his connections had steered work her way while her knack for style and perfection had always impressed those Dennis worked with.

"What about you, Con?" Trevor asked. "Ready for your first year at LSU?"

Conner opened his mouth to reply and then caught the look Rina gave him. He smirked at his older brother and nodded, and though his eyes twinkled with mischief, he kept his response rather tame. "Yeah, I can't wait to get out there. I've been looking forward to going to LSU for ages now. Hard to believe it's finally happening!"

"Yeah, I get it. I remember how I felt when I finally left for college. It was like... exciting but terrifying, you know? I couldn't wait to be living in the dorms and be out on my own, but dang if I didn't miss the big breakfasts Mom always made us on Sunday mornings."

Rina laughed, remembering all the years she had gotten up early on Sunday mornings to cook a big breakfast for everyone. It was the one day a week they all had breakfast together. With everyone's hectic schedules, family dinners didn't usually work out, but she had always made a point of having Sunday mornings with her family.

It really had been strange that first year when Trevor hadn't been at the table with them every morning. And soon, it would just be her. She tried to push that thought to the back of her mind, not wanting to go back down that road.

Conner groaned and rubbed his stomach. His eyes flashed as he grinned at Rina. "You sure you don't wanna come out and visit on Sundays?"

Rina swatted her son's arm, rolling her eyes. There was the common trait all three of her guys had shared—thinking with their stomachs. That was by far the easiest way to get one of them to do something. A good meal had been worth more than all the chore chart stickers in the world when they'd been growing up.

Even now that they were both fully grown, she could still have them wrapped around her little finger just by promising to cook their favorite meals. Rina may not have been a chef, but she had picked up her fair share of skills in the kitchen over the years.

She was going to miss cooking for them once they both went off to school. Not just the Sunday breakfasts either. She wasn't sure she knew how to cook a meal for a single person anymore, especially after cooking for three or four people all the time. Cooking for just herself was going to be nothing short of depressing.

She had always known the boys would eventually go off and have their own lives, but she had always imagined she'd still have Dennis by her side during all of it, the two of them growing old together. Now she'd be growing old alone, and there wasn't much she could do to change that.

Being a widow was awful and depressing. There was no doubt about it.

CHAPTER THREE

The sun had already set by the time they left the restaurant. Street lights illuminated the area, casting shadows every which way. Even without the bright ball of fire beating down on them, it was still hot as could be and would be for at least another month or so. Summer in Florida had a tendency to stick around.

"Hey, Con. Shannon and I are going to meet up with Mark and Ken for a couple of drinks. Wanna join us?" Trevor had his arm around Shannon's waist. Rina sucked in a breath as she watched the two of them, clearly remembering the days Dennis had held her like that.

Conner glanced over at his mother for a moment, then back to Trevor. He chewed on his bottom lip, gears turning inside his head. Trevor's invitation had obviously not included their mother, and Conner was hesitant to accept and leave her alone for the night. She had raised him to be a gentleman, and he hadn't forgotten his manners.

She stood on her toes and then kissed him on the cheek. He had a slight bit of stubble, and Rina wasn't sure she would ever really get used to that. It was hard to accept her baby boy was a man now, but whether she accepted it or not, life moved on either way. "Go have fun. Say hi to the guys for me."

Mark and Ken had been Trevor's best friends growing up, and they had spent more than a few nights over at the house over the years. She could still hear the echoing shouts as they played video games together, along with Conner's whines about being excluded from the group of older boys.

She fixed Trevor with a gaze. He may have quite literally towered over her now, but just one look was enough to make him go rigid. "And you keep an eye on your brother, all right? Remember, he's not quite legal to drink yet."

"Of course," Trevor said quickly, exchanging a silent look with Conner. She had no doubt her youngest would have at least a couple of drinks that night. Heck, if he really was anything like his father, he probably already had a fake ID stashed away somewhere. But as long as he kept it to a minimum and stay responsible about it, Rina had decided what she didn't know wouldn't hurt her.

She assured them she was perfectly capable of calling herself an Uber to get home, but Conner wouldn't hear any of it, insisting she took the keys to his baby instead. It was rare for him to let anyone else drive his car, even family, so she didn't argue too much. Trevor would make sure they both got home in one piece, and this way, she wouldn't have to put up with small talk from a bored driver.

But as the three of them headed off in search of some youthful fun, Rina decided she wasn't ready to go home just yet. There wasn't anything back at the empty house for her to go home to. Instead, she decided a drink of her own was in order. There was a small bar she used to frequent with Dennis not far from the restaurant, so she headed there instead.

On a Thursday night, the place wasn't too crowded. There was a dinge of hazy smoke in the air, but it wasn't nearly as bad as some of the bars she had been to when she was younger. A small jazz band was on stage at the far end, filling the tiny room to the brim with echoing music.

For a moment, she just stood there, taking it all in. She hadn't been there since Dennis had died, but despite not having him at her side, not much had changed. It wasn't like Islamorada, where she knew all the patrons by name or even by sight, but it was familiar and almost comforting.

She made her way over to the bar and slid onto one of the old rickety stools. This place had been here for decades now and the furniture had reflected it. It wasn't dirty or rundown, just worn and well-loved. It was the kind of place locals went after a long day at work to unwind. The people there weren't looking to get laid or hustle games of pool. They just wanted to have a drink and listen to some music before heading home to face their lives.

It was the perfect place for Rina to escape reality for just a little while.

She caught the eye of the bartender, an older man in a blue button-down shirt and jeans. Nothing too fancy, but not too casual either. He acknowledged her with a tilt of his head, and when she ordered a gin and tonic, he nodded in response. His eyes scanned the bar as he made the drink, keeping sight of everything going on.

It may not have been a rambunctious bar, but he wasn't taking any chances. He had been there every single time Rina and Dennis had frequented the bar and yet, she still didn't know his name. Heck, she had only heard him speak maybe a handful of times over the years—which was just fine with her.

She wasn't there to make small talk. She just wanted to sip on her drink and pretend for a little while that her world hadn't fallen apart. Eventually, she would have to face reality again, but for a brief time, she could ignore all the aches and pains.

She had only taken a couple of sips of her drink when someone slid onto the stool next to her. Rina glanced over out of the corner of her eye, taking in the woman's navy blue skirt suit, clinging to her body almost like a second skin. She was easily in her forties, but her hair and makeup and clothes said she was trying to look much younger than she actually was.

"You're Rina Renner, aren't you?" the woman asked. Rina turned to find the woman watching her now, an odd expression on her face. Rina thought about denying it, about ignoring this stranger, but in the end, she nodded and the woman smiled. "I'm Debbie. Debbie Willows. I knew your husband. I'm so sorry about his passing."

Rina stared wide-eyed at the woman, taking her in again. She didn't look familiar, but then Rina didn't know everyone Dennis had worked with or known. She attended a lot of the social functions with him, but not all of them, so it wasn't impossible for this woman to have been telling the truth. Besides, Rina thought, why would she lie about knowing a dead man?

"How are you holding up?" Debbie asked.

Rina shrugged. She didn't much feel like talking about herself, but she couldn't very well be rude either. "As well as can be, I guess."

Debbie nodded, giving her an understanding smile. "You guys had children, didn't you?"

"Two boys, Trevor and Conner."

"They must miss him terribly as well. I've got a girl myself, and I know it's not easy raising kids as a single parent. Though I guess yours aren't really kids anymore, are they?"

Rina laughed and nodded as she took another sip of her drink. It sent a warm wave washing over her as it slid down her throat, slowly chipping away at the weight on her shoulders. "No, they're most definitely not! They're like mountains now. I swear they could pick me up and carry me up a building like King Kong!"

Debbie laughed at the joke and even though the two women had never met before, conversation flowed easily between them. The liquor helped, but at least in Rina's case, she was eager to hear Debbie's stories about Dennis, like those stories might just bring him back to life for a couple more minutes.

"Oh, God, this one time, an intern tripped and sent his drink flying all over the front of Dennis's suit! I thought for sure he was going to flip out, but he just sighed, shook his head, and said he was going to end up buying his dry cleaner a vacation home in the Bahamas at the rate he was going!"

"Oh, jeez, I couldn't tell you how many suits that man went through," Rina agreed. "If he wasn't spilling something on himself, someone else was. Especially when the boys were little, they had no concept of how expensive his suits were, and as soon as he would walk through the door, they always took off running toward him, getting the remnants of the PB&J all over his clothes."

Debbie laughed and nodded. Rina was finishing her second drink and had just ordered water when Debbie had ordered her third drink, the alcohol making them both more vibrant and excited as they swapped stories back and forth. Rina couldn't believe she had never met Debbie before and wished she had met her sooner. They would have been good friends, she figured.

"I swear he was the only man I ever met that dressed to the nines but didn't much care what happened to his clothes at the end of the day," Rina said with a soft sigh. His closet was still full of all of his suits. She hadn't had the strength to get rid of them yet. They were all tailored to fit Dennis, so she doubted they would fit either of the boys, though she figured she should at least offer. "Once, we were on our way home from one of his big company galas. I had on a pretty black dress he had gotten me, and he was wearing a suit that probably cost more than some people make in a month. But when he saw a car broken down on the side of the road, he didn't even hesitate to stop and help the woman change her flat tire."

"He was a good man, wasn't he? Always looking out for other people, never happy, just sitting still and doing nothing." Debbie stared off into space for a moment, an odd expression on her face that Rina couldn't quite place. A moment later, she shook her head as if trying to dislodge a stray thought. "It must be hard now, with two boys in college. I hope he left you enough to pay for it all! I'm dreading trying to pay for Beth's schooling next year, and I've only got the one. I couldn't imagine trying to put two kids through college on my own!"

"He left a good bit behind," Rina confirmed. Dennis had always been fairly frugal with his spending, so she had a good chunk in the bank, plus more from his various investments and his life insurance.

"It should be more than enough for both boys to finish school without any trouble."

Debbie's gaze narrowed for a moment, an odd expression on her face, but when Rina locked eyes with her, it was gone, leaving her wondering if she had seen anything at all or if it had just been her imagination. Or maybe it was the last gin and tonic she had. That seemed to be the more likely answer, Rina decided, and as she stared at her glass of water. She was thankful she had cut herself off a while ago, knowing she wanted to be in the proper shape to drive home.

Conner would not be happy to find out she had left his car in the bar parking lot and called an Uber to get home. His baby was too precious to be left somewhere; it might get a scratch on it. Thankfully it was early in the evening and she'd only had enough to get her tipsy. But the water was already making her little buzz disappear.

Not that she was looking forward to going home early. At least the gin had numbed some of the pain she had been feeling, enough for her to push it to the back burner for a little while. Once it wore off, she'd be right back where she started, staring at the swirling abyss of darkness that kept threatening to overwhelm her.

It took a few moments before Rina realized her purse was vibrating. The jazz band wasn't ear-shattering, but it was loud enough to drown out the sound of her ringtone. She fumbled with the zipper on her purse in a hurry to dig the device out; worried something might have happened to one of the boys. She trusted them, but she was a mother, and she always worried when they went out with friends— especially since losing Dennis.

But it wasn't Trevor or Conner's name on the screen. It wasn't

Shannon or the police or the hospital either. No, it was the one person in the world she wanted to talk to least of all—Holly.

She just didn't take a hint, Rina thought with a grumble. Then, she remembered what Conner had said. Relationships were a two-sided street. And if Holly was repeatedly calling like that, maybe it was something serious. She distinctly remembered the numbness that had washed over her when she had gotten the call about her father's passing, and she prayed Holly's incessant calling wasn't to bring more bad news.

Rina couldn't take any more bad news.

She thought for sure it would make her crack.

CHAPTER FOUR

Rina stared at the phone for what felt like an eternity. The small device weighed like a brick in her hand, but as much as she wanted to ignore it and stuff it back into her purse, she had to find out what was so important. Even if it was bad news, she couldn't run from it forever.

She forced a smile onto her face as she slid off her barstool. She nodded her head in the direction of the bathroom along the far wall of the bar. "I've got to take this. I'll be right back."

Not waiting for Debbie's response, Rina fled toward the women's bathroom. She wove between tables, the patrons not paying her any attention. The people who frequented this bar had tended to keep to themselves. They didn't want to be bothered by anyone else. The bathroom's wooden door swung inwards with a creak, barely audible over the jazz band's music. When it closed behind her, though, it muffled the sound just enough that Rina would be able to hear.

She wrinkled her nose as she looked around the bathroom. It was clean, so far as she could tell, but it was in desperate need of a remodel. The beige paint on the walls had started to chip away, revealing the bare brick underneath. The wooden stalls were scarred and scratched from years of use. There was a pervading stench of stale urine in the air, mixed with the scent of bleach. Not as bad as some of the bad restrooms she had been in over the years, but not exactly a fun place to linger in either.

Taking a deep breath, she held it as she accepted the call. "Hello?" She fought to keep her voice even and neutral. She wanted to snap at her sister for calling when she had explicitly told her not to. But if something really was wrong with their mother or one of their other siblings, Rina wanted to get right to it rather than spending the entire time fighting.

Her body shook slightly as she waited for Holly's response, dreading what she might say. She tried not to fidget but found she couldn't stand still, the nervous energy too much for her to contain.

"Hey, Rina." Holly's voice came through the tiny speaker loud and clear. It was soft and calm, so unlike the sister, she remembered. "How are you holding up?"

Rina snorted, unable to keep the annoyance at bay any longer. "How am I holding up? Oh, so now you care about me and my life?"

"I didn't know about Dennis. I'm so sorry, really. If I had known..."

"Of course you didn't know!" Rina snapped. She could feel the veins in her forehead, throbbing. It took a lot of her self-control not to just chuck the phone at the brick wall. "We're busy with our own lives, remember big sis. That became perfectly obvious once you left the Keys and never looked back. We've got our own lives now, our own families. Things are better this way."

"You don't honestly believe that, do you?" Somehow, despite Rina's outbursts, Holly was still calm and collected. That just pissed Rina off even more. "We're family, Rina. No matter our differences. No matter what we went through in the past. And yeah, I get it. A lot of it was my fault for leaving Islamorada the moment I could, but I was young and stupid back then."

"Just back then?" Rina retorted.

Holly chuckled. "Yeah, okay, I guess I deserved that. Well, I'm certainly not young anymore, that's for sure. Neither of us are, Rina. We're not kids anymore. Don't you think it's time we started acting like it?"

Rina rolled her eyes. Out of everyone in the world, somehow, no one got under her skin like Holly did. It seemed like no matter what her old sister said, it just set her off. But then why shouldn't it? Nothing Rina had ever done had been good enough compared to Holly.

She was the perfect child, the golden child. She was the standard the rest of them were held up to. It didn't matter how successful they became or how happy they were with their lives. None of them had ever been able to compare to Holly.

"I thought moving on with my life was pretty grown-up," Rina said, her voice laced with snark.

Holly sighed. Rina could just see her sister's face in her mind. No doubt, her patience was running thin, just as Rina's was. "Look, I didn't call to fight, okay? I called to invite you to come out to Mom's seventieth birthday party. I know she would really love it if all of us were back home for it."

"Islamorada hasn't been my home in almost thirty years," Rina reminded her older sister. "And I can't just drop everything at the last minute to go back just to ease your conscience, Holly. I have a job here. A family. A life."

The line went quiet. Rina knew Holly didn't want to argue, but she also knew her sister had no leverage to use against her. She had gone back to the Keys only a handful of times over the last few decades. Nothing Holly was going to say would be able to convince her to all of a sudden come back now.

"I'll make sure to send Mom a card. But other than that, I'm done with Islamorada. I'm done with that part of my life, okay? Good night, Holly." Rina ended the call and then stuffed the phone back into her purse. Her head was throbbing now, and it wasn't from the gin and tonics.

Rina took a deep breath, holding it as long as she could with her eyes closed. Of course, the one night she just wanted to forget about all the crap life had thrown at her; the universe decided a chat with her lovely sister was in order. Wasn't that just her luck, though? She never could catch a break, it seemed.

Three long strides brought Rina to the sinks. She flipped the cold water on, then leaned over and splashed some onto her face. The coolness helped ease some of the headache, but she still wished she had a couple of aspirin with her. If it wasn't one thing in her life, it was something else.

On the bright side, she felt much soberer after talking to Holly. Her sister always had been a buzzkill, and apparently, that was still true, this time in a very literal sense. Laughing, Rina shook her head. She was getting too old for this crap, she decided. Late nights at the bar were for people her sons' ages, not her age.

It was time for her to go home and get some sleep.

When she stepped out of the bathroom, she nearly crashed into Debbie. Coming to an abrupt halt to avoid a collision, Rina blinked in surprise. "Sorry! I didn't think someone would be right there!" She tried to laugh off the near accident, but something in Debbie's look made her freeze in place. "Is something wrong?" Rina asked, heart pounding harder and faster.

"Dennis and I had an affair together seventeen years ago," Debbie blurted out. Her face was flushed red, her eyes wide and bloodshot. Had she been that drunk before Rina had gone to the bathroom to take Holly's call? "My daughter, Beth... She's Dennis's child."

Rina stared, mouth hanging open, as she tried to process what Debbie had said. Clearly, the woman had had way too much to drink if she thought Rina was going to find that joke funny. But as she stared into Debbie's eyes, she realized the woman wasn't joking. She was very serious.

There was no way it was the truth, though. That just wasn't possible. Dennis had loved her. The two of them had been happy together. There was no way he would have ever cheated on her. And he certainly wouldn't have had a kid with another woman and kept it a secret! Dennis may not have been perfect, but that was beyond anything he was capable of.

"That's not even a little bit funny," Rina growled. The anger she had suppressed when talking to Holly had bubbled right back up to the surface. Her hands balled into fists at her sides, her nails biting into her palms. She could barely even hear the jazz band playing as the blood rushed to her head. "My husband is dead and you make jokes like that? You've got some balls, lady."

"It's not a joke. It's the truth. Beth is his daughter, whether you like it or not. And she's just as entitled to whatever little nest egg Dennis left behind just as much as you are!"

Rina saw red. Every muscle in her body tensed. She had to bite her tongue just to keep from taking a swing at the woman. She wasn't a violent person, but the accusations this woman made against her deceased husband was more than she could handle right then.

"Piss off!" Rina barked and then pushed past the woman. She didn't even glance back as she made her way through the bar. Her entire body shook with rage, and for a moment, she hoped the other woman would follow her outside, just so Rina could take out some of her aggression.

But she didn't. And soon, Rina had sunken into the soft leather seats of Conner's BMW. She closed her eyes and leaned her head back against the headrest, forcing herself to take slow, deep breaths. She wanted to just go home and crawl into bed, but she needed to let her anger recede a bit before it was safe to drive.

She was completely sober now and really wished she wasn't. But there was no way she was going back into the bar. She never wanted to see that woman again. How she could stand there and make those accusations against Dennis... Just thinking about it made Rina's blood boil again.

By the time she started the car, she was so exhausted, even more so than she had been in a very long time. If she had her way, she would sleep until sometime next week.

CHAPTER FIVE

Groaning, Rina gripped the plush blankets and pulled them up over her head. She squeezed her eyes even tighter, trying to block out the intruding sunlight. Normally she would've been up and drinking her first cup of coffee by the time the sun was up. This morning though, the sun burned into her head, sending pulsing spikes through her entire body.

She shouldn't have drank as much as she had last night. The gin mixed with the stress had given her a hangover like she hadn't experienced since her own college days. It was a not-so-subtle reminder she wasn't nearly as young as she used to be. And she was getting far too old to go out drinking for half the night even if she only had two very strong drinks.

With a groan, Rina gave up on trying to get a couple more hours of sleep. She pulled the blanket down and blinked a few times, trying to get used to the invading light. It took a few more minutes before she had the strength to slide out of bed and crawl to the bathroom to retrieve her bottle of aspirin.

She popped two of them in her mouth and then mustered the courage to look up at herself in the mirror. God, she looked like a train wreck. Her long dark locks were tangled in all directions. The little bit of makeup she had worn yesterday was smudged and smeared, no doubt all over her pillowcase as well. And her eyes... Her normally sharp chocolate brown eyes were bloodshot and cloudy, making it hard for her to even focus on her own image.

"That's the last time I go out drinking," she muttered, taking a quick gulp of water from the tap to wash down her aspirin, then she headed for the shower.

It wasn't until she had stood under the hot spray for a few minutes that she finally started to come back to life. The aspirin had started to kick in as well, and between the two of them, her head stopped pounding just enough for Rina to finally catch her breath.

The shower was big enough to fit at least three or four people. Rina had picked it out herself when they had remodeled the house ten or fifteen years ago. After having had to share a bathroom with Holly growing up and then having to share one with three other girls in her college dorm, Rina was ready to have the bathroom of her dreams. She didn't much care what the rest of the house looked like, but this had been her little haven from the stress of life.

She remembered the mornings when Dennis would slip into the shower with her. Getting clean hadn't been quite what was on his mind back in those days, and just the thought of it sent a flush through her. Without him, the shower just seemed so big. Empty.

She no longer needed a shower that could fit more than one person. She no longer needed a bathroom she could hide in with a glass of wine and a good book, soaking in the equally massive tub next to the shower, when the days got to be too stressful. In another month, Trevor and Conner would head off to school, leaving her alone in the house for the very first time.

Soon, she would have an entire house to hide in.

As Rina came back to life, her brain still sluggish but slowly rebooting, all the details of the previous night came flooding back to her. Going to the bar to unwind with a drink, sitting and talking to Debbie, exchanging stories about Dennis. Then, she remembered what Debbie had said at the end of the night, the accusations she had made against the man Rina loved.

Her hands balled into fists again and she wished she really had slugged her at least once. It would've been the least she'd deserved after ruining Rina's night like that. Then, smacking her forehead, Rina groaned. She had given Debbie her phone number sometime after her second gin and tonic.

The two of them had gotten along so well that she had actually been looking forward to spending time with the woman. God, how could she have been so stupid? How could she have not seen through the rouse right from the start? She was just a gold digger, trying to take advantage of Rina's fragile mental state to pad her own bank account.

By the time Rina finally forced herself out of the shower, she was dreading going back into the bedroom and looking at her phone. But as she wrapped a fluffy white towel around herself, she knew she couldn't ignore it forever.

Steam billowed out of the bathroom when she opened the door. Sunlight still streamed into the bedroom, giving her just enough light to see. Their bed... her bed now, she figured... sat in the middle of the room against the wall across from the bathroom. A California king, it was just another thing that was far too big for just her. Its crimson comforter was wrinkled and twisted from another fitful night of sleep. She would straighten it out before going downstairs, but first, she set her sights on the dark oak nightstand on the left side of` the bed.

There, still plugged into the white charging cable, was her cellphone. With a shaky hand, she picked it up and turned the screen on, letting out a groan when she saw Debbie had already sent her messages. Not just one or two, but multiple messages highlighting just how crazy the woman was.

You can't hide from me forever!
Dennis is her father!
She deserves that money!
You owe us!!!

Rina rolled her eyes as she read each of the messages. Then, she deleted all of them and blocked the number, hoping that would be the end of that craziness. She still couldn't believe the audacity of that woman, trying to use Dennis's death just to get her hands on some of the money he had left behind.

And it wasn't like he left her millions or anything like that. He had left enough to give her a comfortable lifestyle and to make sure the kids would be taken care of, but it wasn't like she was going to be quitting her job and moving to a tropical island somewhere!

Fighting down her anger and annoyance, Rina quickly dressed, opting for comfort over fashion as she slid into a pair of shorts and a t-shirt. She still had a dull headache from the hangover and wasn't in the mood for trying to impress anyone. She didn't even bother with makeup, just brushed her hair out and tied it into a ponytail.

Rina ran her hand along the beige walls as she headed down the hallway. How many times had they repainted them over the years? Light-colored walls and young children hadn't exactly gone well together, but Dennis had insisted on keeping the color, so Rina had insisted he be the one to repaint them every time one of the boys colored on one or crashed into one scratching the paint.

The house was quiet as she made her way down the stairs, stopping to gaze at the spot where Conner had gotten his head stuck between the railings as a kid. All because Trevor had insisted there was no way Conner's head could fit through there. He'd been half right - Conner's head had fit going in, but it certainly didn't come back out. Poor Conner had cried his eyes out until Dennis had managed to unscrew one of the carved wooden bars to create a gap large enough for the boy to remove his head.

No lasting damage, either to Conner's head or the banister, but the poor boy had never lived that one down. Even now, Trevor still liked to bring up that day, just to tease his brother. Rina would have felt bad if Conner didn't have his own arsenal of embarrassing stories starring his older brother.

She paused again in the broad entryway leading into the kitchen. Both of her sons were already in there, along with Shannon. The boys were still dressed as if they had just rolled out of bed, which they probably had. Trevor wore a tattered pair of sweatpants she was pretty sure he'd had for at least five or six years now, but once he found clothing he was comfortable in, it was near impossible to get him to give it up. But he was still a bit more modestly dressed than his brother, who wore just a pair of boxes. Their hair stood up in all directions, and if they'd even run their fingers through it before coming downstairs, Rina would have been surprised.

Shannon, at least, had gotten dressed. She wore a tiny t-shirt tucked into an even tinier pair of jean shorts. The perfect summer attire for Florida and Rina remembered the days when she used to dress like that. Her father used to have an aneurysm each time Rina had come downstairs during the summer.

Which, looking back, was the biggest reason she always dressed like that. Sure, it was more comfortable in the hot Florida summers, but it was mostly because it had driven her father nuts.

Though not as nuts as it had driven the boys! For not the first time, Rina was glad she'd had two boys—boys that she could teach manners to and teach how to treat a woman. With a girl, though? Rina would have been terrified of her getting into all the same trouble she had gotten into in her youth.

Conner was the first one to spot her. He raised his coffee mug in greeting, mumbling his good morning with his mouth still full of toast.

Rina rolled her eyes. Okay, she could attempt to teach her sons manners. But there was a certain amount of piggishness she wasn't sure boys ever grew out of. Even their father had had his moments, usually, after a couple too many gin and tonics, she recalled with a smirk.

"You three look like crap," Rina said with a teasing lilt to her voice. And it was true. Even though Shannon had attempted to look normal, Rina could still see the bags under her bloodshot eyes. All three of them had still been out at the bar by the time she had gone to sleep, so God only knew what time they'd all stumbled home.

"Don't worry, we behaved!" Conner insisted, though his cheeky grin said otherwise. For a brief moment, Rina considered quizzing them about their night, then decided she was better off not knowing. There were just some things that were better off left unsaid.

Still feeling her hangover even after the shower and aspirin, Rina decided to forgo breakfast for a little while instead of pouring herself a steaming cup of coffee. Nothing cut through the haze of a hangover like a good shot of caffeine. At least that was what she always told herself when she was younger.

When her phone buzzed, Rina pulled it out, frowning at it. The number was one she didn't recognize, but she knew who it was the moment she read the message. Number blocked and message deleted, she stuffed the phone back into her pocket.

But not before Trevor noticed. The two of them locked eyes, and he gave her a curious expression. "Everything okay, Mom?" he asked, ever too observant.

Rina forced a smile onto her face and nodded. "Everything's great. In fact, I'm going to head down to Islamorada for a few days. Grandma's seventieth birthday is coming up, and they're having a big party for her. You're all welcome to come, of course. The more, the merrier!"

She wasn't sure where that had come from. She had just told Holly last night she wasn't going to set foot in the Keys anytime soon. And now she was suddenly going back?

The boys knew just as well as she did that wasn't like her. They exchanged a silent look, no doubt saying more with their eyes than they ever could have with words. When they both looked at her again, she saw their concern. No doubt they thought she had finally snapped, that their father's death had finally driven their mother crazy.

And maybe they were right. All Rina knew was she needed to get away from Naples for a little while. She wanted to put some space between her and all the craziness going on in her life for a bit. And while returning to her childhood home wasn't at the top of her list of places to go, at least she had an excuse to go and hide down there.

In the end, they both opted to remain behind in Naples, which was how Rina found herself behind the wheel of her Mercedes, her suitcase in the trunk and gripping the steering wheel with white-knuckled hands, cursing herself for ever going to that stupid bar. Debbie had sent two more texts and even tried to call once, all from different numbers.

Was she changing her number every time Rina blocked her? What was this woman's obsession with her and Dennis? Rina knew her claims of Dennis cheating were lies. She had never once had any reason to doubt her husband's faithfulness.

But that woman had obviously known Dennis well. She had told stories about him at different events, talking like they'd been old friends. If Rina hadn't been so desperate for conversation about her late husband and a bit tipsy, she might have questioned things sooner. But instead, she had just kept on talking to the woman, feeding into her psychotic delusions.

And now she was letting the woman force her back to the one

place she had sworn off. Maybe getting away from the house for a few days would help. It was impossible to turn around in that place without some memory or another being unearthed. And the more distance she put between herself and that lunatic, the better.

Even if it meant bringing herself closer to the siblings she'd worked so hard to distance herself from.

CHAPTER SIX

The soft, steady wind rustled the grass. If it hadn't been for the copious amounts of hairspray she had used, her hair would have been waving as freely as the tiny green blades. Dark sunglasses hid her bloodshot eyes, not that there was anyone around to see them anymore.

Well, no one whose opinions she cared about anyway.

Holly, Randy, and Amy all stood beside her, dressed in dark clothes. Even though the sky was free of all but the slightest wisps of clouds—darkness exuded from the family. Only a few feet away sat the marble slab, with their father's name etched into it along with his birth and death date.

There was an empty space to the right, the place where their mother would eventually rest beside the man she had loved her entire life. Rina stared at that empty space for the longest time, wondering how long it would be until she was back there, watching another freshly dug hole be filled in with dirt.

Rina blinked away tears, shaking her head and forcing herself back to reality. She didn't need any of those morbid thoughts bouncing around in her mind. It had been two years since she'd stood in that graveyard—two years since she'd laid eyes on any of her three siblings.

When she had driven away from the Keys that night, she'd assumed the next time she returned it would be to stand in that graveyard again. That her next trip to the Keys would be her last one, the last tiny thread tying her to the place having finally been cut.

And yet, there she was, speeding down the highway, willingly going back to the one place she had even more memories than her home. Some of them were good memories, she conceded. Mostly the older ones from when she was a kid. But a lot of them were things she would have much rather left buried in the past, thank you very much.

Was avoiding one crazy stalker with money in her eyes really worth dredging up those old memories? It was probably a little late to be asking herself that question, but as she zipped around a tiny Volkswagen Beatle moving about the same pace as its namesake, she decided it was.

Her kids didn't need her anymore. Not in the way they had needed her when they were young anyway. They were both grown now, Trevor heading into his third year of college and Conner into his first. Heck, in the last six months, they had probably done more to keep her steady than she'd done for them.

They were probably glad to have her out of the house for a few days. Knowing Conner, he had probably already started planning a party the moment she'd announced her spur of the moment trip.

With any luck, Trevor would keep him in check and they wouldn't burn the place down while she was gone.

A roadside sign caught her attention. The big blue billboard advertised the local marina, encouraging visitors to stop in for the freshest fish they've ever had. While she wasn't sure of the validity of their claim, she recognized the marina, knowing it was her brother Randy's business.

Out of all of her siblings, he was probably the one who grated on her nerves the least. He was always the easiest one to talk to, probably because he was almost always at least partially drunk and nowhere near as opinionated as their sisters.

Making another split-second decision, something that was becoming a bit too frequent lately, Rina made a sharp turn, just barely making the exit for the marina. She wasn't going to be able to avoid her family while on Islamorada, and if she was going to have to face them eventually, she might as well start with the one sibling who was least likely to bite her head off.

Rina couldn't even remember the last time she'd visited the marina. And yet, as she navigated through the narrow streets, she found herself on autopilot. Even after all those years she had been gone, she still knew the area like the back of her hand. At least, her subconscious did. As long as a tourist didn't ask her for directions anywhere, she was probably safe.

Before she knew it, she had pulled into a parking spot not far from the dock itself. Boats bobbed along in the near crystal-clear blue water, with a handful of men swarming around each one like a group of worker bees, while one little bee, in particular, stood out.

Dressed in a pair of jeans that had most certainly seen better days and a t-shirt that she was pretty sure was blue at one point was her younger brother Randy. Even though she hadn't seen him since her brief visit to the Keys two years ago, she knew she'd always recognize the face of the boy who had driven her up the walls in her youth.

He wasn't a boy anymore, though. Gone was the toothy grin and mischievous eyes. Even though he was two years younger than her, he looked much older. Even from a distance, she could see the stress lines around his eyes. It looked like he was moving slower than he used to, too. The years of drinking must've finally started catching up to him.

If he wasn't careful, he was going to end up working his way into an early grave, just like their father had. Rina was startled by that thought. She'd barely spoken to the man since leaving Islamorada and now there she was, watching him and worrying about his health.

Wasn't that just what she had accused Holly of doing? Swooping in and trying to miraculously save the day? God, she was glad her older sister wasn't there right then. She'd have never been able to live that down.

But still, she was worried about Randy. Just because she hadn't gotten along with her siblings for a long time didn't mean she didn't still care about them. Sure, that caring might've been buried under a couple of decades of resentment, but it was still there, and she doubted it would ever really go away.

She could run from her siblings all she wanted, but she'd never been able to stop caring about the annoying buggers.

With a sigh, Rina killed the Mercedes's engine, threw the keys into the little clutch purse she'd tossed onto the passenger seat. Sitting in the car and staring at her brother wasn't going to do much at all. Besides, it was more than a little creepy when she thought about it.

The moment she opened the door, the sea air hit her square in the face. She froze, taking a deep breath and letting it wash over her. She'd been to the beach plenty of times over the years. It was hard to live in Naples with two kids and not make beach trips a regular part of summer vacation. But there in the Keys, the scent was different. It was more raw, visceral. It was something she had never quite experienced anywhere else in her life.

Maybe coming back wouldn't be so bad, she mused silently. She hated to admit it, but Islamorada did have its charms, which should've been obvious since people from all over the world flocked there every year. But it wasn't the island itself that had kept her away for so long.

It was the people who lived there. More specifically, the ones related to her. One of which was only a few yards away, helping offload crates from one of the boats, completely oblivious of her presence.

Part of her wanted to get right back into her car and leave before he noticed her—that same part of her that had said to forget this stupid and insane idea and just go back to Naples. But after the fiasco the night before when she had trusted her instincts, she decided to just forge on ahead.

Whatever came of this foolhardy trip down Memory Road, she would deal with it later. Either way, it had to be better than staying back at the house, dodging calls from a woman even crazier than her siblings she had left behind all those years ago.

None of the dockworkers even locked up as she slammed the door of the Mercedes shut. But the moment her heels touched the wooden dock, it seemed like every eye was on her. Maybe changing into a skirt and tank top hadn't been the greatest idea.

But even though she felt a bit guilty, it felt good to have so much attention on her. Even at forty-four, she could still draw men's gazes, it seemed. Not that she had even the slightest interest in any of these men, but it was still nice to know she wasn't a complete wrinkled hag just yet. Though Rina also knew if someone like Shannon had been with her, none of those men would have given her a second thought.

A sharp whistle made everyone turn toward the third boat from the end of the pier. A deep bellow of laughter followed as a smirking Randy stepped off the boat and onto the dock, wiping his hands on his filthy jeans. "Well, well, well. Look what the cat dragged in. Didn't think I'd ever see you back here."

"Didn't think I would either," Rina admitted with a shrug. She smirked at him as she looked around at the fishing boats on either side of her, bobbing gently on the waves. The men were back at work, unloading the morning's haul and pretending not to be watching Rina.

Rina barely had time to recognize the look in his eyes before Randy was bounding down the dock toward her like he was still the hyperactive eight-year-old who had constantly been in trouble for bouncing off the walls. She closed her eyes and braced herself, expecting to be barreled over and end up in the water waiting to be fished out by one of the muscular men.

She definitely went flying when Randy collided into her. But instead of ending up splashing into the ocean, she was hoisted high into the air. Strong arms wrapped around her waist as Randy spun her in circles.

Rina found herself giggling uncontrollably, transported back to the days when she used to run and jump into her father's arms, the burly man spinning her around until she thought she might puke. When Randy finally set her back on the swaying dock, and the world around her stopped spinning, she realized just how much he looked like their father.

The realization took her breath away. How had she not noticed sooner? It should've been fairly obvious, even when she had seen him two years ago. Had she really had her head up her butt so far she hadn't seen the resemblance between the two of them?

Or had something else colored how she had seen her little brother?

"I thought Holly said you weren't coming for the party." Randy stood with his hands on his hips, a single eyebrow raised. He may have had Dad's physical looks, but he had somehow managed to pick up their mother's mannerisms, which was impressive considering how often he had complained about their mother favoring her daughters over him.

Rina took a deep breath and held it for a three count. Part of her wanted to just blurt out everything to him – Dennis dying, her constant feeling of loneliness and helplessness, and the crazy woman who had been blowing her phone up all day and making crazy claims. But she kept it all inside, instead just letting out the air in a soft breath.

"Well, I'm here," she said simply, offering him only a shrug in response. Maybe at some point, she would explain everything to him and the others. Probably not, but either way, she wasn't going to do it right there on the docks two minutes after seeing him again for the first time in years.

Randy eyed her for a moment. If she hadn't known better, she would have sworn he could see right through her, right into all those thoughts and emotions she wanted so desperately to keep buried. Before he could say anything, though, a shadow fell over him as a big man walked over and placed a meaty hand on Randy's shoulder.

"Well, aren't you a sight for sore eyes. Didn't think I'd ever see you again, Rina." The man's eyes roamed up and down Rina's body. She suppressed a shudder as his leering gaze lingered on her exposed skin. "I missed seeing you last time you were in town. You sure have grown up since we were kids."

"What a genius you must be," Rina said dryly, unable to contain her snarky remark. Rina wasn't the only one who'd grown up. But despite having grown exponentially in size, Rina still recognized Dean, one of Randy's best friends from their youth and business partner. He had been the one primarily responsible for all the mischief her brother had gotten into back then.

Rina hadn't ever liked him. As a kid, he had just been annoying, even more so than Randy. As they had gotten older, he'd become lecherous, his eyes and hands wandering more than any man's had a right to. And judging from the way he looked at her, that hadn't changed over the years.

Randy shrugged the man's hand off his shoulder. Lips pursed into a tight line, he frowned at Dean, who just grinned at him. Rarely had Rina ever met a man who'd dwarfed her brother. Plenty that was his size and even some bigger, but never anyone who made him look so small.

This man was probably only a couple of inches taller than Randy. But the thick muscle that seemed to cover every inch of his body and the way he looked at the two of them somehow made him appear larger than he should have been. Clearly, he wasn't the runt he'd been anymore.

"Rina," Randy said his attention back on his sister. She may not have seen him in years, but she could still tell when he was forcing himself to smile, and he was most definitely forcing himself. "You remember Dean, don't you?"

"How could I forget? You two still running the business together?" Rina plastered on a smile just as fake as Randy's. Even though she wanted to get as far away from this brutish pervert as she could, she forced herself to be polite for Randy's sake, though she wasn't quite sure why she bothered.

Dean laughed, his deep voice echoing around them. A few of the other dockworkers looked up at the sound, and when they caught sight of its source, they quickly turned their attention elsewhere. Apparently, he still made enemies easier than he made friends.

"When this one decides to grace us with his presence!" Dean patted Randy on the back. He smirked again, but there wasn't any happiness behind it. He looked more like a child with a magnifying glass, getting ready to see just how long it took to roast a line of ants.

Randy took a deep breath, his body stiffening. Then, he glanced over at his friend and nodded. "Speaking of, since I'm pretty sure Rina willingly coming back to the Keys is the first sign of the world ending, I think I'm gonna take the rest of the afternoon off. You guys can handle unloading the rest of the cargo without me."

He didn't even wait for Dean to reply. He took a step toward Rina, then hooked his arm in hers and practically dragged her back the way she had come from. Rina had to fight back the urge to push him away, knowing his grime was getting all over her clothes. Then she decided it didn't matter if she rolled around in the muck with him.

It wasn't like she cared what anyone around here thought of her appearance.

If that was true, she wouldn't have changed before driving down, that incessant voice in her head reminded her. To which Rina promptly clamped down upon it, locking it into a cage and stuffing it into the furthest recesses of her mind.

She didn't have time for an internal monologue that was going to call her out on her mental hypocrisy.

Rina wasn't sure where her brother was dragging her, but since it was away from Dean, she didn't bother questioning him. Her first assumption would be to one of the cabana bars that dotted the area along there.

To her surprise, though, he led her to one of the other docks. This one had just as many boats bobbing in the water, but they were smaller, personal boats rather than the larger fishing and transport boats where she'd found Randy.

He led her to the sixteen-foot speedboat, only a fraction of the size of the one he had been on a few minutes ago. Smaller but faster, Rina mused, remembering all the days she had spent speeding around in little boats just like this one when she was younger. Randy may have been the trouble maker of the family, but Rina had gotten in her fair share of mischief as well.

"Yours, I hope?" Rina teased as Randy held her hand, keeping her steady as she stepped from the dock onto the swaying boat. It wouldn't have been the first time she had snuck away on a boat that wasn't hers, but it had been one thing to do it when she was sixteen and another to do it when she was forty-four. Especially in broad daylight!

Randy smirked at her for a moment. When Rina fixed him with a gaze, he laughed and then nodded. "It's owned by the company, sis. Sometimes, when things are slow, we'll do tours for the visitors, bring in some extra cash, you know?"

He continued talking as he got the boat ready, giving her the latest gossip from around the island. She listened with a smile, once again amused at just how much like their mother he was. A mouse couldn't fart on the island without their mother knowing about it, and it looked like the same could be true for her younger brother.

As Randy expertly guided them out onto the blue ocean, Rina fished her sunglasses out of her purse, sliding them on to keep from going blind. Between the cloudless sky high above them and the reflections of the crystal clear water, it seemed like a real possibility if Rina wasn't careful.

God, when was the last time she'd been out on the water like this? Their father had often taken the family out on the boat he kept docked at the house. She remembered spending many mornings and evenings taking turns diving off the boat and into the water, her siblings laughing alongside her.

Things had been so much simpler back then. Back when just being in close proximity to each other meant they were friends—that they played together, explored together, and camped out under the stars together.

The worst part? Rina couldn't even really pinpoint when everything had changed between them, had gone so sour.

She sighed and leaned back, letting the sun wash over her. God, she'd let their sibling rivalry keep her away from the island for almost thirty years. And yet, she couldn't even really figure out why she disliked her siblings so much, why they fought nearly every time they were in the same room together.

"Remember when Dad busted you for sneaking out after bedtime and stealing the boat so you could have some alone time with that guy you were dating?" Randy's voice interrupted Rina's thoughts. She peaked an eye open to see him glancing over at her, grinning. "God, he was madder than hell that day. That was the same day he had caught me, Dean, and Logan in the boathouse drinking beer. If you hadn't gotten busted that night, I'm pretty sure y'all would have found my body floatin' in the ocean the next morning."

Rina laughed at the memory. She had been up at the Inn with her sisters, helping their mother with some of the housekeeping since their housekeeper had been out on maternity leave. It would have been near the end of her Sophomore year. Maybe a month or two before Holly had walked away from the Keys and never looked back.

And yet, even now, Rina could still hear her father's booming voice as he tore his only son a new one. Dad had always been slow to anger, but when it came to Randy... Rina figured he had always seen the potential in the boy that Randy had never been able to see in himself.

Randy and his friends would've been about fourteen at the time, almost finished with the eighth grade. Looking back, Rina wondered if that had been the start of her brother's road to dabbling in booze or if that was just the first time he had gotten caught.

Back then, though, she hadn't done anything more than laugh

at her brother's latest screw up. Back then, there was only one guy she had really cared about.

"What was his name?" Randy asked, jarring her out of her thoughts again. "Christ, I swear you dated almost every guy in the school back then. I never could keep them straight."

"Shows what a great brother you were," Rina teased. "Weren't you supposed to threaten any boy who even dared look my way? Make some macho threats about what you'd do to them if they even dared to soil my innocence?"

"Ha! You innocent?" Randy gave her a smirk. They had only been out on the water for maybe ten or fifteen minutes, but Rina could already see a difference in him. His eyes were brighter. Even the bags around his eyes seemed to have faded.

"Very funny. Compared to you, I was practically an angel! But to answer your question, it was Steve Trapper I snuck out with that night. And you think Dad was mad at you for drinking? I thought for sure he was going to drown both of us in the ocean that night."

Once they were far away from the shore and the other boats were cruising around the keys, Randy killed the engine, then came and sat on one of the seats across from her. She was just about to say something about wishing she had brought a bottle of water or something when Randy lifted up the cushion of one of the seats, revealing a small mini-fridge hidden below.

When he passed her an ice-cold bottle of beer, Rina took it with a smirk. Leave it to Randy to always have some beer on hand. And even though she should have known better after drinking last night, she popped it open and took a long swing, letting the cool liquid wash over her.

And for a while, they just sat there, staring out at the water as they bobbed along with the current. They weren't terribly far from the shore, and if Rina looked toward it, she could still make out tiny specs the size of ants meandering along the coastline.

"Hasn't changed much, has it?" Randy asked, his gaze watching the little dots alongside her. He took a sip of his beer and then let out a sigh. "Hard to believe this place is almost exactly the same as it was when we were kids, you know? Sure, some of the shops have changed and there's some new faces around town, but mostly? Sometimes, when I walk down the street to the store or to grab some food, I feel like I'm still a kid. I wait to hear Mom and Dad's directions or to hear one of you girls yelling something stupid. It's surreal."

"That's what I'm afraid of," Rina muttered, then took another drink of her beer. Maybe coming back here wasn't such a great idea. Did she really want to drudge up all those old memories again? But then, if she didn't face the past, would she ever really be able to move on from it?

Randy reached out and put a hand on her shoulder. He didn't speak until Rina looked over at him, then he smiled at her. "Holly told me about your husband. I'm so sorry, Rina."

She nodded. Rina had figured Holly would've told everyone, so she shouldn't have been surprised. But she had still hoped she'd have at least a short while before she had to face reality again. But hey, at least her phone had been silent for a little while. Maybe the psycho woman had finally given up.

"You could've come to us, you know. We would have been there for you." Randy squeezed her shoulder. She couldn't look at him this time, though. She couldn't do anything other than try to force down the memories of Dennis that threatened to boil to the surface again. "You're not the only one who's lost their spouse."

"What?" Rina stared at him in shock. Holly hadn't mentioned anything like that when they had spoken. Then again, Rina hadn't really given her much of a chance to. Nor had anyone else reached out to her, not that she could really blame them when she hadn't done any better after Dennis's death.

Randy let out a sigh, then took another long drink of his beer, draining the bottle dry. He leaned over and set it on the floor, then grabbed himself another and popped the top, drinking almost half of it before he looked at Rina again. "At least you got to watch your kids grow up. I've only seen Emma and Sarah a handful of times in the last few years."

Rina winced. Now she remembered Randy and his wife Patty had gotten divorced a decade ago when his girls were still kids. She vaguely remembered rumors of Patty having had an affair, but she had never asked Randy about it.

Debbie's accusations of Dennis having cheated sprung to the forefront of her mind again, and she forced them away. Now was not the time to relive that particular memory. She had enough of them to deal with without entertaining the idea of her husband having been unfaithful.

"I'm sorry," Rina said, eyes downcast. Randy was right. At least she and Dennis had both gotten to see the boys grow up. He may not have gotten to see Conner graduate high school and would miss all the college milestones that were just around the corner, but it was more than Randy had gotten with his girls since the divorce.

Randy let out another sigh and then shrugged again. "It is what it is at this point, you know? It's not like I can go back and change the past. None of us can."

Wasn't that the truth!

"You sure we weren't the twins?" Rina asked dryly. "I always thought you understood me better than the others did. Guess we've got more in common than I thought."

Randy snorted, giving her a smirk again. "Nah, you had a good marriage. I only met Dennis a few times, but he always seemed like a good man. I could tell how much he loved you. Maybe I should've listened to you guys when you had tried to warn me Patty wasn't the right woman for me. It could've saved me a lot of heartaches. No, I think Holly and I are the ones on the same wavelength this time."

"Holly?" Rina asked incredulously. What could little Miss Perfect have in common with Randy? What could she possibly understand about having your marriage fall apart and losing the person you loved?

Randy stared at Rina, his eyes wide as saucers. If he opened them any wider, she thought they might just fall right out of his head. "Shit, you haven't heard?"

"Heard what?" Rina demanded. If she hadn't been sitting down, she would have been the one with her hands on hips, giving Randy the look their mother had always given them when she'd demanded answers for something.

"Jeez, I figured the whole world had heard by now. It was all over the news. Her husband, well, ex-husband, is going to jail for a very long time." When Rina just stared at him with a shocked look on her face, he chuckled and continued. "Turned out he was making a bunch of shady real estate deals behind Holly's back and owed the IRS more money than you and I will probably make in our lifetimes combined. Holly had to testify against him; otherwise, she was going to end up sharing a cell."

"Oh, my God!" That was the only thing Rina could think to say in response. She didn't spend a whole lot of time watching the news, especially not in the last couple of months, so she'd had no idea Holly had gone through any of that.

Now she felt guilty about having snapped at Holly the last two times she had spoken to her. Rina had expected her sister to magically know about the tough time she'd been going through, and all the while, she'd had no idea what Holly had been going through herself. She had again just assumed her sister's life was picture perfect as usual. What an idiot she was.

She was glad Conner hadn't come along with her. Even without him there, she could see the smirk on his face and hear his, "I told you so." Because, of course, once again, her son was right, curse it.

"I guess we've all had our issues," Rina said at last.

And our secrets, she added silently.

CHAPTER SEVEN

RINA COULD HAVE STAYED OUT ON THE WATER ALL DAY. BUT considering the sun was beating down and threatening to roast her if she even thought about staying out there too long, she didn't complain when Randy fired the boat's engine back up and started them on a course back toward the shore.

Except he didn't go back in the direction they had come from. Instead, he kept heading south, and Rina's breath caught in her throat as she realized exactly where he was headed. She opened her mouth to tell him to turn around, to head back to the marina but then clamped it shut.

She couldn't hide from her family forever, no matter how badly she wanted to.

When the Inn first came into view, it took her breath away. Considering how Holly had sounded on the phone a few weeks ago, she had expected the place to be falling down, one step away from being classified as condemned. And yet there it was all two stories, shining like the star of Islamorada it had always been.

Even the cabins dotted along the edge of the beach looked to be in pristine shape. The place most certainly wasn't falling down. Far from it! It looked... just like she had always remembered it from her childhood.

Their father had worked himself to the bone to maintain the place, to keep it looking immaculate. And, more times than Rina could count, he had roped his children into helping with its maintenance.

When she left for college, Rina was probably one of the few girls on campus who could paint, rewire a room, and fix plumbing problems. All of these skills had actually come in handy when Dennis's roommate had gotten a bit too drunk at a party and decided to see just how many socks he could flush down their toilet before it couldn't handle it anymore.

"It's a beauty, isn't it?" Randy asked. He looked over at her, his eyes shimmering with pride. But it was more than just family pride for the Inn.

"You did this, didn't you? Holly said the place was practically falling apart, but it sure doesn't look like it."

Randy shrugged, still grinning. He may not have been a braggart, but he wasn't exactly modest either. "Yeah. I spent a good bit of time up on ladders, repainting the place. But it wasn't just me. Holly busted her butt out there too, and so did some of our cousins. It always was a family effort, you know?"

Heat rushed to Rina's cheeks as she nodded. It had been a family effort and she'd been nowhere to be found. And this time, she couldn't just claim she'd had no idea since she had known.

Holly had called her for just that purpose, and she had snubbed her sister out like a flame.

God, her father, must have been rolling around in his grave. This place had been his pride and joy, and Rina had turned her back on it, just like she'd turned her back on the family. Sure, Holly had been the first one to walk away and not look back, but apparently, she had realized her mistake long before Rina had.

But maybe it wasn't too late to fix her mistakes. Wasn't that something she had always told the boys growing up? That it was never too late to own up to the mistakes they've made and try to fix them. Maybe it was time for her to start practicing what she preached.

Randy slowed the boat as he came closer to the shoreline. Soon, the Inn was right there, and the massive Archer House looming in front of them, just barely able to be seen in the distance. Rina's throat closed again as she stared at it, suddenly wishing she'd had a bit more than beer during their little excursion.

Especially once they neared the dock. Their father's old boat was still tethered there, looking no less fit for fishing or water sports than it had when they had been kids. Either that at least had been maintained, or someone had fixed it up along with the Inn. But that wasn't what really made her heart pound and her hands shake. Up on the shore was an old wooden bench swing. Her mother and father used to sit on that in the evenings, holding hands and watching the sunset together.

But as they neared the dock, it wasn't her mother and father sitting in the swing. Instead, Holly sat there, next to another woman. It took Rina a second to recognize her cousin Cara, and by then, her mouth had gone completely dry. Because of course, she couldn't get a few minutes to even catch her breath and acclimate to being back at her childhood home before she had to face Holly.

She could only imagine how their reunion was about to go. Considering the last two times she had spoken to her sister on the phone, she'd snapped at Holly and then hung up on her. Rina doubted her older sister was going to be thrilled she'd decided to visit the place. And even if she was, Rina knew Holly wasn't going to accept her non-answers about why she had changed her mind like Randy had.

But if she was going to do this, she might as well just rip the Band-Aid off and get it over with, right? Worst case, if it went too bad, she could always catch an Uber back to her car and go home. Heck, this was Islamorada, not Naples. If it really went that badly, she could walk back to her car if she wanted. Nothing was all that far around here, something that would take a bit to adjust to again.

As Randy carefully pulled the boat next to the dock, Rina fought the urge to slink down in her seat. Instead, she stood and helped him get it tethered. Then, she accepted his offered hand and let him help her onto the dock. She turned and offered him a hand as well, though she knew he didn't need it. But it gave her an excuse to look away from the end of the dock where her sister was already making her way toward the pair of them.

Rina had barely managed to turn back around when Holly was right there in front of her. Rina's eyes went wide, and she braced herself, fully expecting Holly to shove her into the water for how rude she had been when they'd spoken last. But instead, when Holly's arms lashed forward, they wrapped around Rina instead of pushing her away. Awkwardly, Rina hugged her back, wondering if all the stress Holly had been through with her ex-husband had finally cracked the eldest sister's brain.

"You liar," Holly said with a laugh. "I bet you did that on purpose, didn't you? You couldn't just say you were coming. No, you had to go and surprise us! God, we'll be lucky if Mom doesn't have a heart attack when she sees you!"

Rina shrugged, giving Holly a half-smile. She felt a bit guilty at lying to her sister like that, but she didn't quite want to dive into everything just yet. Being back here was already threatening to overwhelm her at any moment, and she figured baby steps were better than diving in too quickly and drowning. Because once Rina got started on explaining everything, she would have to get it all out, and she definitely wasn't ready to lay her soul bare just yet.

Once Holly finally released her, still without shoving her into the ocean, thankfully, Cara stepped up to hug her as well. She had always gotten along with her younger cousin. They had all been so close at one point during high school. It was so nice to see her again, and at least seeing and talking to Cara didn't dredge up nearly as many uncomfortable memories as her eldest sister.

"The guys are going to go nuts when they see you. I'm pretty sure they both had a bet going on when you'd come back here." Cara smirked, her eyes twinkling. Something told Rina she'd had in on that bet and she just might have been on the winning side of it.

Holly clapped her hands together, making everyone jump a bit before they turned to look at her. A sheepish smile on her face, her brown eyes shone in the bright sunlight. Somehow, she looked completely different from how she'd been at their father's funeral. It was like she had become a completely different person since then. Maybe she had. Randy had only told her the basics of what

Holly had gone through, but that much of an upheaval had to have an effect on a person.

Heck, Rina wasn't the same person she had been before Dennis's death. She was still figuring out who this new person was, but she knew she wouldn't ever be able to go back to who she had been before. Part of her had died the day Dennis had, and that part wasn't coming back any more than he was.

Maybe that was why she had come back here, Rina mused to herself. She'd come into adulthood here on Islamorada, set herself on the path to become the woman she'd been. It was only fitting she come back here to try and figure out where to go now.

"I think we need to have a special dinner to celebrate!" Holly cheerfully exclaimed. Rina raised an eyebrow at her sister's enthusiasm. Here she had thought Holly would be upset about her showing up out of the blue, and now there she was, practically throwing her a party. "I'll give Chef Stevens a call and have him whip up something special for us. And you and the guys have to stay and join us, of course." Holy directed the last part to Cara.

"Guys?" Rina asked, an eyebrow raised.

"Jason and Paul," Cara explained. "They've been doing the bulk of the remodeling work on the Inn. They've got their own construction business, so anything that required more skill than a simple handyman, they've been handling."

Rina nodded. She remembered Cara's brothers, though she hadn't known they had their own construction company. That certainly explained why the Inn was looking a lot better than how she'd imagined it. While she had no doubt, Randy could be pretty handy if he put his mind to it, and she knew Holly had been taught the ins and outs of taking care of the place just as she had, if things really had been as bad as Holly had made it out to be, they would have needed professional help. Now she knew where they'd gotten it.

Holly stepped away for a minute to make her phone call, and Randy gave Rina a nudge. "Why don't you give me your keys? I'll take the boat back to the marina and then bring your car around for you. Give you girls a chance to catch up."

Rina frowned at her brother. She didn't like his plan one bit. While he took the boat back to the marina, Rina would be left alone with Holly and Cara. And while she had no problems with Cara, she wasn't so sure she wanted to be left with Holly. Just because Holly hadn't yet tossed her into the ocean didn't mean she wouldn't get around to it. But it wasn't like she could just flat out refuse Randy's offer without being rude, which he no doubt knew.

"Sure. But if you scratch her, I swear they'll never find your body," Rina threatened as she pulled the keys out of her purse and tossed them to her brother. The look she gave him told him if he dawdled, she would murder him no matter the state of her car when he returned.

Randy grinned and winked at her, then hopped back into the boat and untied it, pushing away from the dock just enough to fire up the engines and speed off. Rina stood there, hands-on-hips and lips pursed as she watched him disappear from view. Wasn't that just like her brother to leave her alone with the one sibling she would have been happy to avoid all?

Well, she wasn't completely alone, at least. Maybe with Cara around, they might just be able to keep things civil.

At least, that had been her hope.

But when Holly returned, still smiling and looking full of

energy, Rina wasn't sure if civil was what she should've been aiming for. Rina couldn't remember the last time she'd seen Holly acting like this. It had to have been back when they were in high school, at least. Holly had always seemed fairly happy on the few occasions they had seen each other over the years, but never like this.

Now she was... giddy was probably the best word Rina could think of to describe her older sister. As Holly and Cara led Rina on a tour of the Inn, showing off all the things they had done to bring the place back to the land of the living, Holly spoke in an animated and excited tone.

"God, you should've seen the cabins," Holly said with a mock shudder. "It was amazing they hadn't been condemned before we got to work on them! I don't think they'd even gotten basic maintenance since Dad had died."

Cara glanced at Rina and then rolled her eyes. "Oh, please, it wasn't that bad! They were structurally sound still, which was pretty impressive considering how old they are and how rough the storms can be here. But when your father built something, he built it to last. They were just ugly and in much need of being brought into the twenty-first century. I'm pretty sure the stoves in them were older than I am! And, I mean, the things still worked fine, but God were they ugly!"

Rina and Holly both laughed. While Holly had clearly been exaggerating just how much things were falling apart, Rina was pretty sure their cousin was just as bad when it came to how old and ugly things were too. Then again, maybe she wasn't. Rina thought back to how the cabins had looked when she'd been a girl and if they really hadn't been updated since then...

Yeah, they definitely would have been on the uglier side of the scale.

Her father loved the Inn and really had put his heart and soul into the place. But while he may have been capable of building cabins that could withstand multiple hurricanes, a sense of fashion and design was not exactly his strongest point. Their mother had been better about things, but unless she'd changed a good bit since back then, her sense of decor was still firmly set in the 1970s.

Not exactly modern.

And while most of the visitors liked the charm of a town that hadn't changed a whole lot over the last thirty years, they had also come to expect certain modern amenities. Like cable TV and the Internet, something Rina distinctly remembered her father kicking up a stink about installing. He'd been old fashioned to the core, and his idea of an Island vacation involved the beach, the water, and all the natural beauty Islamorada had to offer. To him, TV and the Internet were a needless expense when the visitors should've been perfectly happy exploring the island!

"I take it Mom isn't nearly as hard to win over as Dad had been when it came to changing things?"

Holly and Cara exchanged a look, both of them looking their fair share of guilty. "Well, let's just say it's easier to ask forgiveness than permission," Holly finally admitted, which made Rina laugh.

"God, you should've seen your mother's face when she saw all the new paintings in the rooms!" Cara said, practically cackling at the memory.

As they wandered the grounds, Rina wondered why she had been so nervous about seeing her sister again. So far, things had been just fine between the two of them. Maybe it was just because

Cara was there as a witness. Or, just maybe, Holly had been serious when she had talked about putting the past behind them and moving on. Rina still wasn't sure what she thought of about that idea, but she figured it was at least worth a shot.

It sure seemed like a better option than constantly being at each other's throats.

By the time Randy returned, it was nearly dinner. Of course, the butthead had taken his sweet time getting back. He had changed clothes, she noticed, now wearing a clean pair of faded blue jeans and a button-up shirt. When Rina glared at him, he just grinned at her, giving her a slight shrug.

He'd called her bluff, and if things hadn't gone so well between her and Holly, she might have actually taken out her annoyance on him. Instead, she just whispered a promise to pay him back for disappearing on her, which just made him grin even broader.

Her little brother had gotten a bit cocky in his old age. She would have to find a way to remind him he was still at the bottom of the sibling totem pole.

That thought shocked Rina. When was the last time she'd thought about her siblings like that? It really was like a dose of nostalgia had hit her square in the face and she'd been transported back in time to being a kid. Randy was being an annoying butt and she was debating the best way to get her revenge on him. She couldn't help but smile to herself.

What was it about this place? Rina wondered as they headed toward the main building of the Inn. It hadn't been like this the last time she had visited. Then again, maybe it had. Maybe it'd been her that had just been too stubborn to realize it.

A long table had been set up outside of the Inn grounds under a large palm, a pair of servers bustling around it as they set out plates, silverware, and glasses. A glance over at Holly only earned her a smirk and a shrug. When Rina had teased about throwing a party, she hadn't realized just how close to the truth she was!

Her cousins Paul and Jason were already there, leaning up against the wall of the Inn, joking and laughing about something. When their small group walked up, both men glanced their way, then let out low whistles, their eyes locked on Rina.

"Well, I guess Cara really was telling the truth," Jason said with a lopsided grin. He shook his head as he stared at his cousin. "The world really must be ending if Rina Archer is back on the Island."

"Rina Renner," she corrected with a smirk of her own. Her husband may have died, but she still had his name.

Jason just rolled his eyes at her correction. "Doesn't matter what you call yourself. You'll always be an Archer."

Rina pursed her lips, mulling that over in her head. Six months ago, if someone had said that to her, she would have rolled her eyes and probably smacked them but now... Maybe still being an Archer wasn't such a bad thing. Like Holly had said, they weren't kids anymore. Why should they keep letting petty arguments from decades ago keep them apart?

"Really? You had to send one of the staff to come let me know we'd be making a family dinner behind the Inn tonight? One of you couldn't have taken the time to walk over to the house and tell me in person? Or just pick up a phone and call me?" Nelly Archer's cracking voice echoed around in the open air.

Everyone turned at the same time to see the delicate woman walking across the manicured lawn toward them. Rina's breath caught in her throat as she looked at her mother, shocked at just how frail she looked. It wasn't that she hadn't believed Holly when she had called and told her about her mother being sick; she just couldn't have ever imagined her mother looking like... that.

God, Dad's death must have been harder on her than Rina had realized. Combined with the stress of running the Inn and everything else, Nelly Archer had most definitely seen better days in her near seventy years.

Guilt kicked Rina in the gut. Her formerly rumbling stomach now threatened to unload the breakfast she'd had hours earlier. How could she have been so stupid? How could she have let herself get so caught up in petty drama and siblings feuding that she had neglected her own mother?

She could only imagine how she'd have felt if Conner and Trevor had done that to her. She wasn't sure she would ever be able to forgive herself for not having been there. She knew better than any of the others how devastating losing your husband was. And poor Nelly had gone through that all alone, without even her children to give her comfort.

"We figured it was better to surprise you." Holly moved to stand next to Rina as she spoke. Then, hand on Rina's back, she guided her younger sister forward.

Nelly froze in place. She leaned forward, squinting, her eyesight not what it once was. Even with Nelly still a good twenty feet away, Rina heard the sharp intake of air. And then, after a long moment, Nelly launched herself forward. The small woman moved faster than she should have been able to in her condition. But before Rina could even so much as move a muscle, Nelly was right there in front of her, wrapping her skin-and-bones arms around Rina's waist.

"Oh, sweet Jesus!" Nelly cried as she threatened to break Rina in half with her tight grip. "First, Randy and Holly, and now you! It's so good to see you, baby. I'm so glad you decided to come out for a visit."

"Hey, Mom. It's so good to see you. How're you feeling?" Rina smiled at her mother, the guilt still gnawing at her insides. She had swallowed the lump that was in her throat. She was going to have to find a way to make it up to her, somehow.

"Oh, don't worry about me. I'm doing just fine. How are you? Holly told us about Dennis's passing." Nelly gave her daughter a look that only someone else who had suffered the same loss could. Nelly was the one person who knew exactly what it was like to lose the love of your life.

Why hadn't Rina reached out to her sooner? How could she have been so stupid, wrapping herself in self-pity and resentment that she couldn't even bring herself to call her family? Maybe the last six months would have gone differently if she'd had Nelly to talk to. Maybe then she could have helped her mother before it got this bad.

"I'm doing as well as can be," Rina admitted. Part of her wanted to bare it all right then and there, but she bit her tongue. "I wouldn't say I'm doing great, but I figure I'll get there eventually."

"It never goes away, but it does get easier with time, honey," Nelly said with a nod. Then, she glanced around at the assembled group of family members. "Just remember you're not alone. That's the biggest thing you can do for yourself."

Rina nodded. She wasn't alone, and that was something she had told herself almost every day since Dennis had died. He'd been such a major part of her life, but he wasn't the only thing. She still had her boys, at the very least. And, just maybe, she still had other family she could lean on too.

Their little intimate moment was interrupted then by the clatter of the rear door opening. A contingent of servers marched out, arms laden with trays of food. Everyone took that as their queue to find seats around the long table that had strings of fairy lights that hung from the palm trees above. It always looked so beautiful at nighttime. Then they all settled in just as the large platters were placed on the table in front of them.

Chef Stevens had really outdone himself this time! Arranged before them was the biggest selection of freshly cooked seafood Rina had seen in many years. Just watching the servers place the food down had her mouth-watering and stomach growling. The guilt still gnawed at her insides, but for a brief while, her hunger overpowered everything.

Rina noticed an empty chair left next to her elder sister and wondered who could possibly be missing. She didn't have to wait long to find out, though. Just as they started helping themselves to the plethora of food they had been gifted with, a familiar figure walked over and slid into the open chair.

Wide-eyed, Rina watched as Holly and Jake Holton exchanged smiles. She remembered the two of them dating back in high school, and Rina had been pretty sure they were going to end up married. But when Holly had gone off to college without looking back, she had left him behind as well.

Now it seemed they'd rekindled a bit of the passion they had shared way back when. From what Randy had told her, Holly's relationship had gone down in flames, and Rina was glad to see her sister wasn't wallowing in a pit of depression. That was a sinking feeling Rina knew all too well, and she wouldn't wish that on anyone, even the sister she had despised for so many years.

Everyone expressed their condolences over the meal, but Rina was thankful they didn't dwell on Dennis's death for too long. They did spend a good bit of time asking about him and their boys, though, and Rina happily shared memories from over the years.

A small voice in the back of her mind likened the meal to the previous night when she had swapped tales with the woman who had turned out to be a psycho, and Rina hoped she wasn't about to have a repeat performance. She dismissed that voice, though, trying to move past her petty emotions.

She had spent too long keeping her family at arm's length. It was time for her to start trusting them again, at least until they gave her reason not to.

Losing a loved one was a life-changing event. Maybe, if she played her cards right, she might be able to get something good out of her loss. She had to at least try, right?

When dinner ended, most of the extended Archer family headed to their respective homes for the night. Rina, however, followed Holly and Nelly back to the Archer house, her heart once again racing as she struggled to believe she was really there, really back at her childhood home. Willingly, too. At least, most willingly.

Nelly quickly excused herself to bed, giving each daughter a hug. Holly invited her to share a glass of wine, just the two of them, but Rina decided she wasn't quite ready to tempt fate that much just yet. Instead, she carried the suitcase that Randy had so kindly brought inside for her upstairs, following behind her older sister.

But when Holly opened the bedroom door, Rina could hardly breathe. It was the same bedroom she'd slept in nearly every night until the day she had left for college. And while Amy had clearly decided to impose her own sense of decor over the place once Rina had moved out, it still looked very much the same as it had the day she'd left.

Her Motley Crue and Bon Jovi posters still hung on the wall over her bed. She wouldn't have been surprised to open the dresser and find faded jeans with the knees torn up and t-shirts from the handful of concerts she had been to growing up. Her eyes went to the ceiling, fixating on a tile directly above where her head would lay on the bed, and she wondered if teenage Rina had left anything behind in her secret hiding place.

"See you in the morning," Holly whispered, slipping off to leave Rina alone in the past.

CHAPTER EIGHT

WAKING UP IN HER CHILDHOOD ROOM WAS MORE THAN surreal. When she slid out of bed and opened the curtains to let in some sunlight, she half expected to hear Amy groaning and complaining about the light. Amy had never been a morning girl, which had made sharing a room with her a trying experience to say the least. Rina had never been one to be up before sunrise, but to Amy, the only appropriate time to wake up was noon.

The whining didn't come, though, and Rina was able to pad her way down the hall to the bathroom and get herself ready for the day. By the time she arrived downstairs, Holly was already there, dressed in a light pink blouse and capris, sipping a steaming cup of coffee.

"I hope there's more of that," Rina said after a low moan, eying the ceramic cup Holly clutched protectively.

Holly nodded toward the coffee pot on the counter, still three-quarters full of the succulent brown liquid. Rina practically salivated as she poured herself a glass, adding just a hint of milk and a scoop of sugar. Then, she leaned against the counter and gently blew on the cup, trying to get it down to a drinkable temperature.

She so badly wanted to guzzle it right then and there, but she really didn't want to burn her mouth first thing in the morning. That would just end up leaving her crankier and more irritable than she normally was in the morning.

"So, you mentioned a party for Mom?" Rina asked, keeping her eyes on the tantalizing drink. Almost there, she thought to herself.

Holly nodded as she turned in the old wooden chair. She still clutched her own cup, sipping at it almost teasingly as she eyed her younger sister. "I've got the invitations all written up. I've just got to deliver them around town without Mom finding out."

Rina snorted, giving Holly a half-smirk. "Good luck with that. Mom may not have looked great last night, but if I know her, she's still keeping her thumb on the island's pulse. It's gonna be hard to get something like this all planned and ready to go without her catching on beforehand."

"And that's why I'm being extra careful about it. Cara's got the invitations with her, so Mom won't accidentally find them lying around the house. And I figure I'll make some excuse to slip away from working the Inn today and hit the town to give the invitations out."

"You don't think Mom is going to wonder why you're gone all day? Because if I know you, you've invited almost the entire island." The red tinge that rose in Holly's cheeks told Rina she was right. "That's not something you can slip out and handle in a couple of hours. So unless you've got a really good excuse for where you're going to be all day, Mom's not gonna fall for it."

Holly pursed her lips. She wasn't quite glaring at Rina, but she definitely wasn't thrilled about Rina trampling around on her little parade. Not that Rina had ever minded ruining Holly's plans before, but she was supposed to be trying to mend their issues, not spark another war.

They weren't girls fighting over boys anymore. They were grown women who were supposed to be planning a surprise party for their mother. Rina being right wouldn't just hurt Holly. It would ruin the surprise for their mother, and she didn't want to be right that badly.

"Well, do you have a better idea then?" Holly asked at last. Rina could hear the strain in her voice. She was struggling to stay neutral and not devolve into their normal bickering just as much as Rina was.

Frowning, Rina took a tentative sip of her coffee. It wasn't quite cool enough to drink yet, but it didn't immediately scald her either. She hated trying to figure out dilemmas like this before she'd had her first cup of coffee. There was a reason one of her employees had gotten her a mug for Christmas last year that said, "Coffee first, then questions."

"I'll do it," Rina said, looking up to meet Holly's surprised gaze. "I haven't been back to Islamorada since Dad died. If I tell Mom, I want to go out and explore the town and catch up with some old friends, she's not going to question it."

"Seriously? But you said it yourself; it's going to take all day. Do you really want to spend your entire day going door to door, inviting every person Mom knew to her party?"

Rina took a deep breath and then shrugged. So it wasn't the best idea she had ever come up with, but it was a far cry better than Holly delivering the invitations, at least if they wanted to keep it a secret from their mother. "It's not like I've got anything else planned. Why not spend the day delivering invitations? It'll be better than getting stuck painting rooms or something here."

Holly frowned at Rina, fixing her with a gaze only a mother was capable of. Rina was pretty sure Holly saw right through her weak excuse and knew darn well Rina just didn't want to sit around the Inn with their family all day. Burying the hatchet was one thing, but that had to be done slowly. Too much time around her family and she was liable to say or do something she would regret.

"Then why don't we split the invites? I'll do half and you can do half. Mom won't question it if I have to leave the Inn for a couple of hours. I can tell her I'm meeting some friends or looking at new carpeting for the Inn or something. Then neither of us will have to spend all day going around town."

Rina couldn't argue with that plan. It certainly beat wearing her shoes out by walking from one end of the island to the other. She may not have been ancient, but she wasn't a kid anymore, and she didn't quite like the prospect of going to almost every house on Islamorada.

Because of course, their mother had to know almost every single person who lived in town.

Holly pulled up her master list of invitees and then divided it in half, each of them taking one half of the island. Rina wasn't exactly looking forward to trekking across half the island, but it was the least she could do for her mother. After essentially abandoning her after her Dad had died, Rina wanted to do anything she could to make her mother's birthday as successful as possible.

Cara met the two of them at the restaurant for a quick breakfast, providing them with the stacks of invitations they'd both be delivering. As Rina stared at what looked like an endless pile of papers, she had to keep reminding herself she was doing this for her mother.

Rina briefly considered driving instead of walking, but she knew that would just end up making it take longer. Islamorada wasn't that big of an island and with the number of places she would be stopping at to deliver invitations, driving just wasn't practical.

When she knocked on the first door, the older man who opened it stared wide-eyed at her. "My goodness, if it isn't Rina Archer. I wasn't sure I'd ever see you again in this lifetime. What brings you of all people to an old man's doorstep?"

Rina smiled at Mr. Fletcher. He'd been her high school gym teacher. And while he was perfectly pleasant to talk to now, she could still hear that friendly voice turning into shouts as he "urged" the students to run faster as they did laps around the school's track.

When she had told him about the surprise party for her mother, the man looked overjoyed. Apparently, since he had retired from teaching, he hadn't had much to do, and he quite liked the idea of a surprise party.

"I'll be sure to keep quiet about it," he said with a wink. "I doubt Mr. Floofers is going to go telling too many people, though."

Rina suppressed a giggle as she thanked the man for his discretion. Then, she was on to the next house, and then the next house, and then the house after that. Rina knew almost every person she dropped off an invitation to, to some extent or another. They were former teachers, aging parents of her school friends, or just friendly faces that would have been living on Islamorada since before she was born.

Not much really had changed since she had moved away. Sure, there were a few new faces among the crowds and the familiar ones had aged significantly. But at the end of the day, it was the same small village it had always been. And Rina doubted it would ever really change—at least, not within her lifetime.

It was a little before lunchtime when she knocked on the next door on her list. To her shock, it was Alexandra Summer— one of her childhood best friends who had opened the door. The two women stared at each other for a long moment, eyes wide and neither saying a word. Then, they both leaped forward and embraced each other, squealing the entire time.

"Oh, my God! I can't believe you're back!" Alex gushed, sounding like a schoolgirl. "How long have you been here? And why didn't you call me the moment you arrived?"

Heat rushed to Rina's cheeks as she tried not to look too guilty. Truth be told, she hadn't even thought of calling up her old friends. It was more than a little selfish of her, but to her credit, with everything going on, Rina wasn't exactly thinking straight lately.

"I just arrived yesterday and got wrangled into spending some quality time with the family. You know how it is."

"Oh, of course!" Alex smiled as she nodded.

"What's going on out there?" a familiar voice called from inside. Rina froze as Samantha Palmer came around the corner into the hallway directly behind Alex. Her eyes widened when she saw Rina standing in the doorway, and she let out a squeal of her own as she rushed over to hug her friend. "Oh, my God! What are you doing here?"

Rina laughed as she hugged her friend. When she had agreed to deliver the invitations for Holly, she hadn't intended on running into her two childhood best friends!

Alex invited her in, and the three of them sat around her small kitchen table sipping on iced tea while Rina filled them in on her mother's seventieth birthday party, giving each of them one of the endless stack of invites. "Hey, at least now I've got one less house to visit! You guys being together saved me a trip up a driveway!" Rina said with a laugh.

"Right? I swear it's impossible to throw any kind of party on this island without inviting everyone." Sam gave her a sympathetic smile. Her eyes were alight with amusement, though, which earned her a smirk from Rina.

"How's the shop going?" Rina asked, leaning back in her chair as she eyed the two of them. She remembered them going into business together, opening a bridal shop on the island. It had been amusing way back when and that all three of them ended up working with weddings.

"Other than having to deal with a non-stop stream of Bridezillas, it's been going great. There's never a shortage of people who want an island wedding!" Alex gave her a wolfish grin. Rina could only imagine how much the brides and grooms were overpaying just to have the tropical wedding of their dreams. The island was only so big and could only accommodate so many weddings each year, which meant each one paid a premium for their spot. And judging by the look on Alex's face, the premium extended to things like their dresses, too!

Rina laughed and nodded. "It's the same in Naples. I swear if there's one thing that's universal, it's how horrible brides can be when it comes to planning their weddings! Though, to be fair, even the worst bride doesn't compare to most of the mothers and mothers-in-law I have to deal with. It's not even their wedding and they've still gotta have their fingers in everything!"

"Ain't that the truth!" the two chorused at the same time, making everyone burst into laughter.

Sitting around the table getting caught up, Rina found some of the stress of the last few months starting to fade away. When was the last time she had gone out with friends or just sat around talking and laughing? Heck, when was the last time she'd even seen most of her friends. They had all treated her as if she was made of glass recently, walking on eggshells like she just might crumble to dust if they said the wrong thing.

She hadn't told Alex and Sam about Dennis yet, not wanting to spoil the mood. Eventually, she would have to tell them, of course, but she was afraid of just how much things might change once she did. She didn't want to go back to being treated as if she were breakable, thank you very much.

"Oh, crap!" Alex said suddenly, eyes fixed on the clock hanging on the wall above their heads. "It looks like our lunch break is over. We're gonna have to get back to the shop."

Rina nodded, fighting back the urge to sigh. She'd been enjoying their company, and she wasn't ready for it to end just yet. But she couldn't exactly just ask them to take off work. Nor could she really afford to just sit around chatting. Not if she wanted to avoid an angry Holly. She still had at least half of her stack of invitations to hand out, after all.

"Our last appointment should be done by around three," Sam said. "Once you're done handing out all your invitations, meet us at the shop. We're taking you out tonight!"

Well, Rina certainly liked the sound of that! A girl's night out? One where she would actually be treated like a real person and not a glass doll? She was more than ready!

CHAPTER NINE

By the time she finished handing out her entire stack of invitations, Rina was more than ready for that night out with the girls. Rina was even positively sure her sister had completely cracked. Planning a party for this many people was going to be one heck of a headache, and she wasn't quite sure Holly understood that. Not that everyone would show up, of course, but if even only a fraction of them did, it was going to be a very busy day.

She headed back toward downtown, finding Alex and Sam's shop easily. She paused outside, looking at the gorgeous wedding gowns they had displayed on mannequins in the large glass window at the front of the shop. The one on the left was more traditional, with more white fabric than anyone in their right mind would wear in the Florida heat.

The one on the right, though... It was gorgeous. The top was sleeveless, with an A-line cut made from lace. Even on the hottest day, the bride wouldn't be sweating more than normal. The lower half was made from thin layers of flowing silk. It was more than enough for modesty while still allowing the wearer to breathe.

That was the kind of dress you needed to get married in on an island in the Keys. Heck, that style would've been preferable anywhere in Florida, unless you weren't ever planning on setting foot outside in your dress. But Rina knew from experience just how insistent people could be on being as traditional as possible. Not that it stopped them from wanting to get married on the beach instead of inside a church, though.

But Rina had also learned not to even try arguing with them. It just wasn't worth the headaches that it would cause. It was better to let them do what they wanted, then try to fight back laughter as they sweat buckets under the intense sun that threatened to roast them alive in their bulky dresses of endless fabric.

A tiny bell chimed above the door, announcing Rina's arrival when she walked inside. Sam stuck her head out through curtains near the back, searching for the source of the noise. When her eyes landed on Rina, she grinned and nodded. "We're still finishing up. Make yourself comfortable, and we'll be out as soon as we can!"

Rina nodded and wandered around the shop for a few minutes, checking out the various dresses the girls had on display. They truly were works of art, and Rina wished they weren't so far away. She would have loved to have steered her clients here instead of some of the prissy and stuck-up shops around Naples.

A couple of chairs were placed near the back, with a small table in the center. Rina grinned when she noticed the piles of wedding and bridal magazines. She scooped one up and then made herself comfortable in one of the chairs. It had been six months since she'd worked a wedding or any other event, and she hadn't kept up with the latest trends as much as she should have during her bereavement leave.

She flipped through one of them, checking out the latest styles. She probably had all the same magazines stacked up in a pile at the house since she had her own subscriptions of them. But until now, she hadn't been in the mood to even glance at them. It was hard to get excited about weddings when you were dealing with the loss of your spouse.

Seconds later, a loud shriek made her jump and nearly drop the magazine she'd been reading. Rina stared at the cloth curtains separating the dressing area from the rest of the store. "Oh, my God! Are you serious?"

When the meltdown continued, Rina tossed her magazine back into the pile and then stuck her head through the curtain. The woman Rina assumed to be the bride-to-be was at the far side of the room, pacing back and forth as she spoke to someone on the phone. She wore a floor-length gown. Not quite as big and bulky as some of the dresses the shop sold, but not nearly as light and fashionable as the one Rina had been admiring either.

Rina turned and met the shocked gazes of Alex and Sam. She slipped inside and walked over to them, giving each of them an inquisitory look. Moments later, the woman stopped yelling on the phone and slumped against the wall, sobbing as she listened to whoever was on the other end.

"The dress fits perfectly. And it's exactly what she asked for," Sam said in a whisper, staring in horror as the woman continued to spiral downward.

Alex nodded her agreement. "She was perfectly happy a few

minutes ago! She took a couple of pictures in the mirror and sent them to someone, then her phone went off and... this happened."

"Maybe it's the groom calling off the wedding," Sam suggested, looking at the woman with a forlorn look. It wouldn't have been the first time Rina had seen that happen, and judging by the looks on their faces, they'd seen it happen as well. Sometimes it just wasn't meant to be.

Finally, the bride ended the call. The phone fell from her hand and clattered against the floor. She stayed sitting, legs pulled up against her chest, and continued crying.

Rina sighed and shook her head. An upset bride wasn't anything new for her. And while Sam and Alex had dealt with brides before, they didn't have the long-term relationship with them like Rina did. Once they had finished the dress, they were no longer involved. Rina often saw the weddings from start to finish, and they didn't always have a happy ending.

"Come on. Let's get her changed out of the dress and see if we can get her calmed down." Rina glanced at the woman again, pursing her lips. She so badly wanted to ask what had gone wrong, but she knew better. There was no good answer to come from prying into the personal life of a Bridezilla.

After getting the woman's name from Alex, Rina walked over and squatted down next to the woman. She handed her a couple of tissues, which she accepted gratefully, dabbing at her eyes. "Guess it's a good thing I didn't have any makeup on this time," Avery said with a sad smile.

"That's why I always suggest doing the makeup last. And preferably with a professional makeup artist. Trust me; eyeliner does not come out of these things!" Rina smiled at her, hoping to put the woman at ease. When she offered Avery a hand, the woman took it, then let Sam and Alex help her back out of the dress and into her street clothes again.

Once she was fully clothed, she looked down at the cell phone, still lying where she had dropped it. She sighed, then squatted down and picked it up. When she turned to look at the trio of women, she smiled shyly, and then her gaze dropped to the floor. "I'm sorry about... that. My wedding's on Saturday and my wedding planner just backed out after getting into a massive fight with my mother." She took a deep breath and then rolled her eyes. "Not that I can really blame her. My mother can be... a handful. I'm just not sure what I'm going to do about the wedding now. It's not like I can just call up another planner at the last minute! They book up months in advance, if not years!"

"Well, I hope you're at least getting your money back!" Sam said with a short laugh. "If she's the one who bailed, you should at least get a refund. Even if it was because your mother is a handful."

Avery winced, then sighed and shrugged. "I guess I'll have to call and find out. Because otherwise, I'm really screwed. Not only will I have to find another wedding planner at the last minute, but then I'll have to figure out how to pay them!"

Rina took a deep breath and held it. She chewed on her bottom lip, mulling the idea over in her head. Finally, she let out the breath and figured to hell with it. She had been acting on impulse and instinct since she had decided to come back to Islamorada. Why not keep it going?

"I'll do it," Rina said, to the shock of everyone in the room. She smirked and shrugged, then fished a spare business card out of her purse and handed it to Avery. "If you can get the money back from the other planner, then great. Otherwise, don't worry about the fee. When you call her, have her send me everything she's done so far and I'll take it from there. This close to the big day, almost everything should already be in place anyway."

"Are you for real?" Avery stared at her with big, wide eyes. She looked like she was either going to have another meltdown or burst out into song and dance. Rina wasn't sure which. Then she turned her gaze to the business card and started nodding. "I'll talk to my father and give you a call. And don't worry; I won't let my mother interfere this time. There's a reason my parents got divorced when they were younger."

Crisis averted, the woman practically skipped out of the bridal shop. Sam and Alex carefully put the dress back into its protective bag and then hung it in the back. Apparently, they charged a bit extra to store the dresses before the wedding; this way, the brides wouldn't have to worry about any unfortunate accidents beforehand.

They really had their business down to a T!

CHAPTER TEN

ONCE THEY HAD FINISHED PUTTING EVERYTHING AWAY, SAM and Alex whirled on Rina, arms crossed in front of their chests. They pursed their lips at her and then glanced at each other as if they were trying to figure out who should be the one to chew her out.

"Oh, just spit it out!" Rina said with a roll of her eyes.

"Why would you offer to take over that woman's wedding for free? You're a professional! You shouldn't be doing things for free!" Alex fixed Rina with a glare like she was a mother chastising her child. It was a look Rina was very familiar with, having been on the receiving end of it from her own mother many times and from having used it on both of her boys.

Rina glanced over at the door. Sam had locked it after Avery left, and the three of them were now alone for the foreseeable future. She'd been planning on holding off on telling them about the last six months of her life until a little later, but now was as good a time as any.

"I haven't worked in six months," Rina told them, earning shocked looks from both friends. "Dennis died; he had a massive heart attack. At first, I just... I couldn't even think of trying to work, you know? But then it just became easier to sit and wallow in my pity instead of trying to face the world. But I like my work. I miss it. And I figured this was as good a chance as any to dive back into it."

Neither of her friends spoke. They just stared at her like she'd suddenly sprouted two more heads. Then, before Rina could blink, they launched themselves at her, hugging her until Rina thought she was going to suffocate.

"Oh, my God, why didn't you tell us?" Alex demanded.

Sam was right there, chastising her as well. "You should've called! We would have come up and helped; you know that!"

Rina's cheeks flushed crimson as she stared at the ground. Why hadn't she called her friends? Sure, they weren't as close as they'd been as kids and teenagers, but they were still her best friends, weren't they? Certainly, no one else had ever come along and usurped that title.

And yet, she couldn't help but feel like she had abandoned them. She'd been the one to leave without looking back. She had neglected their friendship just as much as she'd neglected her family. What right did she have to go crawling back to them for comfort?

"That's it. This calls for margaritas!" Alex declared. And before Rina could even think of a way to respond, they had dragged her out of the bridal shop and down a couple of blocks to the little bar frequented mostly by locals.

As Rina sipped on her margarita, she stared up at the bar where a couple of people sat chatting with the bartender. She still remembered sitting at the bar back in Naples, the woman coming up and preying on her weakness. Maybe if she'd called Alex and Sam when Dennis had died, she would have never gotten into that position.

She thought about telling them about her crazy stalker and the wild accusations she'd made about Rina's late husband, then decided against it. They didn't need to be bothered by crazy unfounded rumors any more than she did. Besides, it was better to just try and forget the woman. It wasn't like anything she said was even remotely true!

Alex and Sam dragged the rest of the details of her past six months out of her, though, offering her the comfort she should've sought out way back when. To her surprise, though, they didn't immediately start treating her as a fragile object. They just treated her... normal. Even though they now knew the loss she had suffered, the way they spoke to her and acted around her hadn't changed even a bit.

Rina smirked as she drained the last of her margarita. That was what friendship really was, wasn't it? They knew exactly what she needed and weren't afraid to give it to her. Which just made her feel even more guilty for having neglected them for so long, though they didn't show any signs of caring.

Talking to them was like they'd been apart for a couple of days, not a couple of years.

God, she had missed her friends!

"You should've brought the boys down with you!" Alex said with a laughing grin. Her eyes twinkled in the low lit bar, the flush in her cheeks, showing just how much the tequila had started to affect her. "Although, I'm not sure they'd be ready for Edith and Ella! They'd probably have those poor boys wrapped around their fingers in no time!"

Everyone laughed at that, and Rina wasn't so sure her best friend was wrong. Well, maybe when it came to Trevor. He was devoted enough to Shannon that he most likely wouldn't be swayed by a couple of college girls in bikinis.

Conner, on the other hand... Yeah, he would have been drooling like a starving puppy. Girls were probably his single biggest weakness, and from the stories Rina had heard about Sam and Alex's daughters, they knew just how to work a boy to get what they wanted.

"I'm surprised Jonathan survived the two of them!" Rina said with a laugh, referring to Sam's son. He would've been about the same age as Trevor if she recalled correctly.

"Who said he did?" Sam smirked and flagged down a waitress for a fresh round of drinks. "Those girls knew just how to work him growing up. You'd have never known he was older than both of them. But then, it was always two against one. Sometimes I swore Edith was Ella's sibling and not Jonathan! Though I'm sure, she had certainly wished for that plenty of times over the years!"

Rina laughed, but her heart ached as her friends continued talking about their daughters. Rina had always wanted a daughter, and though she loved her sons with all of her heart, she still couldn't help but be a little jealous. She had never got to do the mother-daughter things she'd gotten to experience with her own mother. And while she had done her best to pass things on to the boys, none of them were particularly interested in learning to cook or bake beyond what they needed to feed themselves. None of them had any interest in interior design or fashion. She had never gotten to sit and talk about teenage gossip and which boys at school had caught her daughter's eye.

Not that she minded the days of going out in their backyard and tossing around a football with the boys or helping them plan the perfect first date for a new girlfriend. She cherished those memories too, but she still wished she could've gotten the best of both worlds like Holly had.

Rina wasn't sure how many margaritas she ended up having—probably too many if she had to hazard a guess. But at least this time she didn't have to worry about driving home! Plus, she wasn't alone, either. And on Islamorada, she didn't have to worry about wandering home at night, more than a little drunk.

Alex insisted on paying their tab, despite Rina's protests, so she declared their next night on the town would be on her. Something about this wicked grin both friends gave her in response said she might well regret that promise, but she was far too drunk to care.

Besides, an expensive bar tab was well worth it for friends like these. They'd stayed by her side, no matter how long they'd been apart. She couldn't have asked for more and wasn't going to let them go easily. Not for a second time, anyway!

They stumbled out of the bar into the cool night air, laughing their heads off. Rina took a deep breath, taking in the salt air that permeated the island. You were never far from the water on Islamorada, and you could tell just from breathing in the air. God, she had missed this, Rina realized.

She had done everything she could to get away from her

siblings and in return, she'd distanced herself from everything she had loved about living in Islamorada.

"Let's go for a swim!" Sam declared, thrusting her fist into the air. She grinned at Alex and Rina like she had just come up with the best idea on the planet.

Rina and Alex glanced at each other, both sharing the same concerned look. Then the margaritas took over and they both agreed, making their way to the closest beach access.

"Wait. I don't have a swimsuit!" Rina said as they made their way through the soft sand. That sudden realization made her stop in her tracks, the other two stopping a few feet ahead and turning to look at her.

"So? Neither do we!" Sam said like that should've been obvious.

Alex nodded her agreement. "It's not like we've never gone without swimsuits before! Besides, is there really that much of a difference between a bikini and underwear anyway?"

Rina took a deep breath and held it, considering Alex's words. She wasn't sure if it was the margaritas or if just being around her friends again had reverted her to being a rebellious teenager, but she found herself shrugging off her concerns and catching up with her friends.

Moments later, they had all shed their outer clothes, stripping down to just their undergarments. Illuminated by the moon and stars, they ran laughing into the waves. Normally crystal clear, without the bright light of the sun to illuminate the depths, the water was near pitch black, threatening to swallow the three of them whole.

But they had all grown up on Islamorada. They all knew the water's secrets and how to navigate its terrain. They had spent many nights together, swimming under the stars and letting their problems of the world wash away. She'd nearly forgotten those memories, having let them become buried in the back of her mind beneath the resentment she'd had for her siblings.

"God, I was such an idiot," Rina declared, shouting her words up to the heavens.

"You said it, not me!" Sam answered with a laugh. Then, she thrust her hands forward, sending a small wave of water cascading toward Rina, hitting her in the face and filling her mouth with its saltiness.

Rina sputtered as she spat out the water. Then, she glared at her friend. Not that Sam could make out the look in the darkness, though Rina was certain her friend had gotten the message. And if she hadn't, then the splash of water Rina sent surging toward her a moment later certainly got it through loud and clear.

And then, the war was on. It was every woman for herself as the three friends competed to see who would come out as the Queen of the Waves. It was a game they'd played when they were children and full of energy, constantly splashing and trying to dunk each other until, one by one, they gave up, leaving only one girl standing as Queen.

But they weren't kids anymore and were a heck of a lot more stubborn than they'd been before. They were a heck of a lot drunker too, which probably hadn't helped. Rina lost track of time before they finally called a truce, declaring themselves all Queens before stumbling toward the shore, each one gasping for air.

"God, we're not as young as we used to be, huh?" Alex asked with a laugh. She collapsed down onto the sand, her body coating itself in the soft yet coarse grains. "But dang, that felt good!"

Sam and Rina nodded their agreement and flopped down next to her. There were beach showers not far away, so they all ignored the sand clinging to every inch of their exposed skin.

"We should've brought towels," Rina said as she leaned back to lie in the sand. She stared up at the massive blackness dotted with specks of light. The view of the sky from Islamorada was more raw and unfiltered compared to Naples. It was both awe-inspiring and terrifying at the same time.

How many nights had she laid on the beaches here, just staring up into the sky? Usually, with a boy next to her, she remembered with a laugh. She couldn't even remember the names of most of them. For a while, she'd gone through guys like they were candy.

It was amazing how much had changed and yet how much had stayed the same.

"I should probably get back to the house soon," Rina said with a sigh. Even though she wasn't a kid with a curfew anymore, she knew she'd be getting a ton of questions about where she had been all night—if not from her mother, then from Holly. And now that she had burned off a lot of the alcohol during their roughhousing, she was thinking about it more rationally.

Sam sat up suddenly, making Alex and Rina look over at her with raised eyebrows. Sam's lips grew into a wide, toothy grin as she started nodding to herself. "You can't go home yet. There's one last thing we need to do before we call it a night."

Alex and Rina glanced at each other. Neither of them had any clue what their friend was going on about, so they just shrugged before turning their attention back to Sam.

"Fish tacos!" Sam declared with a wicked laugh.

Rina was about to declare her friend had finally gone insane when her stomach growled its approval. Everyone went silent and then burst out into laughter. Rina nodded to her friend, fully ready to admit defeat. She was hungry, after all. She hadn't eaten much since lunch and between the margaritas and horsing around in the ocean, she was more than ready to devour a few fish tacos! Maybe a few dozen, at the rate she was going.

The girls wiped as much sand off themselves as possible, then headed up to the beach showers. They all shrieked as the ice-cold water cascaded down upon them. Laughing, they danced in and out of the spray, trying to rinse themselves clean without freezing into popsicles.

"We still don't have towels!" Rina reminded them, and she was not looking forward to putting her clothes back on while dripping wet.

"My car's at the shop," Alex said with a shrug. "It's only a couple blocks away and I've always got towels in the trunk. If we hurry, we can get there, dry off, and then get dressed before too many people see us!"

Sam nodded her agreement with that plan and then added her own suggestion. "And then, we can drive to that little drive-thru taco shop that's just at the edge of the island. The one that's open all night that we used to go to when we were teenagers?"

"That place is still around?" Rina asked incredulously. Though, really, she shouldn't have been surprised. Not much on the island had changed, after all. And that place had always been popular with teenagers. There were only a handful of places open later that weren't bars, and Rina figured even this generation of teenagers needed somewhere they could go to satisfy their late-night munchies!

Even though Rina thought dashing a couple of blocks toward Alex's car was one of the silliest ideas she'd heard in years, that didn't stop her from following her friends along the sidewalks, all of them trying to suppress their laughter. Islamorada didn't quite roll up the sidewalks at dusk, but it also didn't have a bustling nightlife either.

There were a few clubs and resorts that kept the restless tourists occupied, but the locals tended to call it a night fairly early. But of course, they still had to dodge a couple of groups of drunken tourists and a small contingent of local teens out to let loose a little before they'd made it to the little Honda still parked in front of the dark bridal shop.

True to her word, Alex had a whole stack of towels in her trunk. Again, she shouldn't have been surprised. Rina had always kept towels and an extra set of clothes in her car when she'd lived there. You never did know when a spontaneous trip to the beach was in order! And, while she had grown out of that sort of thing once she had left, apparently her friends hadn't. But, then again, why would they? Island life was far different than living in Naples

"Now, how about those fish tacos?" Sam said as she adjusted her blouse. They'd mostly dried off, but their clothes still clung awkwardly and would for at least a few minutes. Sam pulled a hair tie seemingly out of thin air, and then tied her damp hair up into a high ponytail.

"Okay, but it's my treat!" Rina declared, eying both friends. They had paid for her drinks. The least she could do was feed them! And if she was the one paying, she wouldn't feel guilty for devouring as many tacos as she had planned.

Plus, being the one treating had the additional advantage of getting the shotgun seat, so Sam was the one who got stuck sitting in the back. And by the time they left the drive-thru and found a place to park where they wouldn't be disturbed, they had enough fish tacos to feed a small army or three ravenous women.

By the time Alex pulled the car back onto the road and headed toward the Archer house, Rina would've been surprised if there was even a crumb left in the car. They had devoured far more tacos than they probably should have, but while Rina was pretty sure she was going to have to roll up the stairs to her bedroom, she was happier and more content than she had been in the last six months.

CHAPTER ELEVEN

Rina grinned and waved as her friends drove off. She could only imagine what Sam would tell her husband about where she'd been. The three of them had spent the entire evening acting like teenagers again, and Rina was almost sad it was over.

But her friends had responsibilities. Though Sam's youngest and Alex's daughter was both eighteen, they both still had to be mothers. And while Alex was long divorced, Sam also had a husband at home that was bound to be waiting for answers.

As the taillights of Alex's silver Honda faded into the darkness, Rina let out a sigh and shook her head. She could only imagine what her own sons would have said if they'd been there to witness their mother coming home smelling like a combination of booze, saltwater, and fish tacos.

She was about to turn toward the house and head inside when she heard a noise in the distance. It was like a dull thudding sound, followed by what sounded like muttered cursing. Holly hadn't mentioned anything about someone working late that night, but then Holly hadn't exactly shared the ins and outs of the Archer Inn with her either. She was only there for the party, after all, and she didn't need to be clued into the exact inner workings that went on around there.

Still, though, she couldn't just walk away and ignore the sound. This was her family home, after all. If someone was sneaking around that shouldn't have been, Rina wanted to know about it. More than that, she was going to put a stop to it. Islamorada didn't have much trouble with crime; at least it hadn't when she had lived there, but there were always outliers or bored teenagers getting into trouble.

Either way, Rina was ready to put a stop to whoever was causing that commotion.

Making her way in the direction of the beach with all the bravado the last remnants of her margaritas could provide, Rina felt as if she were walking on air. It didn't take long before the location of the noise was in sight - the boathouse sitting at the base of the dock. A single man was out there, moving boxes from out of the boathouse and into the back of a large speed boat.

Rina frowned and picked up the pace. If someone thought they could just waltz onto Archer property and make away with supplies, they were about to get a bit of a surprise. But as she came closer, she recognized the man. She couldn't remember his name to save her life, but he had been one of the workers at the dock Randy had introduced her to when she'd first shown up.

He froze in his spot when he caught sight of her. Then, he must've realized who it was. He continued on his journey, sliding the cargo into the back of the boat with a handful of others. "Rina, right?" he asked as he dusted his hands on his pants.

Rina nodded as she ran her gaze up and down the man. He was dressed much as he had been at the docks, dirty coveralls and an even dirtier t-shirt. She was starting to wonder if any of the guys who worked at the marina bothered washing their clothes. But then again, if they were constantly going to get covered in gunk, Rina supposed their wives might not want all that crap clogging up their washing machines.

"Dale," he said when Rina raised an eyebrow at him. He grinned at her and extended his hand, then glanced down and realized it was still dirty and shrugged. "We met at the marina yesterday. I work for your brother, Randy."

Rina nodded. She pursed her lips as her eyes drifted over to the boxes he'd loaded into the hull of the large boat. "I remember..."

Dale nodded toward the cargo Rina had been eying. He chuckled and then shook his head. "Your brother ordered a bunch of stuff for the marina but put the Inn's shipping address in for some reason." He rolled his eyes in a dramatic fashion and then shrugged. "But he's the boss, so when he tells me to go fix his mistake, I just get to bark and go pick up a bunch of crap in the middle of the night."

Well, that certainly sounded plausible. Randy always had been a bit air-headed growing up. And if the rumors she had heard were true, he was drinking enough to kill a herd of buffalo these days. Rina could only imagine that wasn't helping him keep things straight.

"I'm guessing this isn't the first time he'd screwed something up?" Rina asked, wanting to confirm her own suspicions.

The man, Dale, looked a bit guilty as he nodded. "It's been getting worse lately, I think. He's a good man, and I hate to talk bad about him, but I think the drinking might be starting to get to him."

That was exactly what Rina had been thinking. She made a mental note to talk to her brother before she left, see if she could help steer him back on the right track. Having some drinks to take the weight off your shoulders was one thing, but it really sounded like Randy might have crossed the line into addiction. And if that was true, she wanted to at least try to help him out.

She left Dale to finish loading up his cargo, wandering down the dock to the quiet beach as she mulled everything over. She really didn't want to butt into Randy's life and try to tell him how to live it. That had always been Holly's job, not hers. And she also didn't want it to seem like she was judging him for the choices he'd made. She knew all too well how easy it was to make mistakes and let grief send your life spiraling downward.

But if Randy needed help, if he wanted help, then she was going to make sure he knew she would be there when he was ready.

She had been walking for a few minutes when girlish giggles caught her attention. She looked up to see a couple standing at the edge of the water. It looked like they were skipping rocks on the waves, and Rina smiled, figuring it was a couple of the guests from the Inn out enjoying the quiet evening.

But as she came closer, she realized it wasn't guests. It was Holly! And not only that, it was Jake Holton standing there with her! Talk about surprises... she thought to herself. She was just about to turn around and head back to the house, give them their space when Jake looked over and spotted her.

"Rina, is that you?" he called, his voice echoing clearly across the beach.

Welp, so much for that plan! Rina thought with mild annoyance as she waved to the couple. "How's it going?"

Rina watched as Holly narrowed her eyes at her as she came more into view. Her lips were pursed, giving a look Rina was more than familiar with by now even if she hadn't seen it in quite a while. "You're out late," Holly noted, her tone more than a bit accusatory

"So are you," Rina shot back. Eyebrows raised as she fixed Holly with a look of her own. She wasn't just a little sister anymore. She was a mother in her own right, perfectly capable of looking chastising.

Holly's ego deflated a bit as she nodded. "Jake stopped by and we decided to go for a walk along the beach since it's so nice out tonight. Did you have any trouble delivering all the invitations?"

"Not a bit," Rina said with a smile. She had been perfectly happy when they were all done, but it hadn't been any trouble—just tiring. "Ran into Alex and Sam, actually, which is why I'm so late getting back. They insisted on the three of us going out for a girls' night."

Old habits really did die hard, Rina thought with a snort. There she was, a grown woman with two grown kids of her own, and she was still explaining herself to her older sister. And she couldn't even blame Holly for it this time. It was just habit to try and defend her actions, one she had apparently not grown out of.

She didn't, however, go into details about her girl's night. She figured Holly didn't need to know she'd drank enough to go for a moonlit swim in her underwear, which was still slightly damp.

"Nothing like reconnecting with old friends, huh?" The furtive glance she sent Jake's way told Rina exactly which of her friends Holly had been most enjoying getting caught up with.

Rina turned and looked out at the endless sea of darkness in front of her. It wouldn't be too long before the sun started to peek over the edge of the horizon, but for now, it was as dark as ever. "I don't think I've ever seen a view as gorgeous as the Keys," Rina said, glancing over at her sister. "Sunrise, sunset, even the middle of the night, it doesn't matter. Just standing at the shore, gazing out for what feels like eternity... I almost regret the boys didn't get to grow up experiencing it like we did."

Holly stepped away from Jake and came to stand beside her sister. She, too, stared out at the water, letting the sight wash over her. "Yeah, I know what you mean. I kind of wish I'd gotten to raise mine here, too. Gabby was here not too long ago, and she marveled at just how gorgeous it was."

Rina nodded, fully understanding. She had seen the look of shock and wonder on many tourists over the years. And while she'd never truly been able to understand it growing up, she understood it perfectly now. As a kid, Islamorada hadn't been anywhere special. Tourists had flocked there, sometimes spending a fortune on their vacations. But to Rina, it had just been home.

It wasn't until she'd moved away until she had been gone from her home for so many years that she finally understood the magic and charm the island had. It was no wonder people from all corners of the world descended upon the place every single year. There truly was no place like Islamorada.

"How's Gabby doing? And Sean?" Rina asked. She couldn't really remember the last time she had seen her niece and nephew.

Probably at her father's funeral two years ago, though she barely remembered interacting with them.

"Sean's good. Happy. Gabby's pregnant though and due to be married soon," Holly said with a smirk. She knew Holly's son already had a daughter, but it was easy to see just how happy she was that Gabby would be having a child as well.

She was a natural mother hen. She always had been. With their parents always so busy taking care of the Inn, a lot of the household duties had fallen to Holly, and she had been a natural at it, even if Rina had resented her when she was younger.

"Boy or girl?" Rina asked.

"It's too soon to know, but Gabby said she doesn't want to know even when it's possible. She wants to be surprised in the delivery room." The roll of her eyes and shrug told Rina Holly didn't exactly agree with that decision. But she was also resigned to it, knowing it was ultimately Gabby's choice and not hers.

"Trevor's been dating this girl Shannon for a while. She's really a sweet girl. Perfect for him. He insists they don't have any serious plans for the future, but I've seen the way they look at each other. I'll be surprised if there's not wedding bells ringing soon!"

Holly laughed and nodded. "They always think we're blind, don't they? Guess we were the same way with Mom and Dad, though. We always thought we were sneaking around in their blind spots when we were really right in the open."

"Ain't that the truth."

Jake chuckled on the other side of Holly. He glanced over at the two of them and then smirked. "I'm pretty sure that's a universal fact. I'm sure my two thought they were pretty sneaky with the things they tried to get away with growing up. It makes me wonder just how much my parents were aware of but never told me about!"

Everyone laughed, and just like that, the little bit of tension that had been hanging in the air had been broken. Then Holly tossed a couple of rocks to Rina, and she joined them in their rock skipping as they all three told stories of their kids' hijinks.

By the time Rina made it back to the house and up to her room, she collapsed onto the bed, more than a little exhausted from her long day. But she also felt more alive than she had in a very long time. Even before Dennis had died, she hadn't quite felt this free and at peace with the world.

She should have come back here ages ago. God, she still couldn't believe she'd been so stubborn for so long. Sometimes it really did amaze her how much wiser her kids were than she was.

Rina forced herself back out of bed to change her clothes and brush her teeth. Even though her underwear was still slightly damp and smelled like seawater, she very easily could've just closed her eyes and gone to sleep. But she was a grown woman, not a twenty-one-year-old stumbling home after going on a bender. Tomorrow morning, when she inevitably woke up with a hangover, she would thank herself that she'd done at least the basics to get herself ready for bed.

When she fished her phone out of her purse to plug it into the charge, she glanced at the screen and noticed a text had come in while she had been out swapping stories with her sister and her old/new boyfriend. She pressed her thumb to the reader and then immediately regretted it as the message appeared on her screen.

You can't hide from me.

CHAPTER TWELVE

Rina's head throbbed as she pulled the pillow out and placed it over her eyes to escape the sunlight peering in from behind the curtains. Even though the margaritas had almost completely worn off by the time she'd made it back to the house last night, that hadn't stopped her from getting another major hangover. When was she going to learn she was too danged old to stay out all night drinking?

And the fish tacos... They had been delicious the night before. Now though, her stomach ached, telling her that had been another major mistake. At the very least, she shouldn't have had nearly as many as she had. Jesus, when was she going to learn?

Despite her urge to remain in bed and sleep off her hangover, she forced herself to get up and shower. The hot water, and the Aspirin she fished out of the medicine cabinet, once again helped her return to some semblance of normal. But what really helped kick the hangover in the teeth was the pot of fresh coffee once again waiting when she made it downstairs.

Holly wasn't there this time, though, and Rina figured she was already up at the Inn. It wasn't exactly late in the day, but it wasn't early anymore either. Rina had slept in for the first time in ages, somehow managing to sleep through the sunrise.

She was sitting at the table, sipping on her coffee and reading the news on her phone when it started buzzing. She frowned at the unknown number on the screen, remembering the text message from the previous night. Maybe it was better to just send the call straight to voice mail.

Rina sighed and shook her head. If it was that crazy woman, Rina would just have to give her a piece of her mind.

"Hello?" Rina said after pressing the green accept button.

"Hi, is this Rina? Rina Renner?" a light feminine voice asked. It was a familiar voice, but not the nasally voice of the woman from the bar.

"This is her..."

"Oh, good. This is Avery. We met yesterday at the bridal shop?"

"Oh, yes! I remember." Rina sat up, smiling. She had known the woman would call at some point, and she should have figured it would be sooner rather than later since her wedding was right around the corner.

"Well, if your offer is still good, I was wondering if you'd be free to meet with my father and me so we can go over everything for the wedding?" The woman's voice was tentative, like she was afraid Rina would yell at her. Was she always this timid, or had her call with the previous wedding planner just gone that bad?

"Absolutely. I'm free pretty much all day today. Just let me know when and where would be a good place to meet up."

They spoke for a few more minutes, making plans to meet up at a little beachside restaurant that was known for having delicious breakfasts. Despite the lingering effects of the hangover, Rina's stomach was growling by the time she ended the call.

She headed upstairs to find her tablet, amused at just how many times Avery had assured her that her mother would play no part in the planning of the wedding from here on out. Not that Rina really needed the assurances. She had dealt with her fair share of pushy mothers in her years working as an event planner. She knew just how to placate them and get them to go away.

She sat on the edge of the bed on her tablet, putting together a folder of photos from some of the previous weddings she had worked. Even though she was doing this pro bono and the bride-to-be didn't have any other choice than to use Rina's services, she still wanted to prove she wasn't just some hack from off the streets.

Then she dug out a simple sundress from her luggage. It wasn't anything fancy, but she hadn't exactly planned to be working when she'd packed her belongings. This had been a spur of the moment trip, meant to be a vacation for the most part.

But, eventually, she would have to get back to work. At least this was a way for her to dip her toes back into the water instead of just diving headfirst like she usually did.

The little breakfast place Avery had suggested wasn't too far from the Inn. Compared to most of the businesses around town, it was brand spanking new. In reality, it had opened up while Rina had been away at college, so it'd been there for a couple of decades now. But to the locals, if a business hadn't survived into at least its second generation of owners, it was still new.

It was a fairly tiny place and practically bulging at the seams with the sheer number of people they had managed to cram in there. The locals all knew to get there early and most did since they had to be at work in the mornings anyway. But the tourists tended to meander in at all hours of the morning. They were on vacation, after all, and Rina was one of the few people who was up with the sun even when she wasn't working.

It didn't take more than a moment to spot Avery. Mostly because the moment she stepped into the little bistro, Avery had let out a squeal. She hopped up from the table she had been sitting at and sprinted over to Rina, wrapping her arms around the older woman.

Rina stared with wide-eyes at the sheer exuberance this girl exuded. What had happened to the quiet, almost timid girl she had spoken to earlier? This was like the girl had just taken a heaping helping of speed. She stumbled over her words as she thanked Rina profusely for saving her wedding even though Rina hadn't done anything just yet.

She was in a daze as the woman dragged her back over to the table she'd been sitting at. She was still trying to figure out what she had gotten herself into when the man at the table stood up, jarring her attention.

Rina sucked in a breath as she stared at the familiar face. Her mouth went dry, her hands shaking slightly.

"Rina, this is my father," Avery said, though Rina barely heard the words.

"Steve..." Rina could barely get the word to form on her lips.

This was a man who needed no introduction. Not to her, anyway. She knew Steven Trapper better than almost anyone on Islamorada. At least, she had.

Now though, after almost three decades, she wondered just how much had changed in the boy she had fallen in love with so long ago—the boy who'd swept her off her feet and then broke her heart into a million pieces.

"So the rumors really are true. Rina Archer has returned to Islamorada..." Steve's voice was deep and melodic, just like she'd remembered it. No, not exactly the same. She could hear the subtle differences from when they'd been younger. But, if anything, his voice had become even more mesmerizing.

"Rina Renner," she quickly corrected, holding up her hand to display the golden band still wrapped around her finger. She had spent the last six months debating whether or not she should continue to wear the ring or not. Now, she was glad she had kept it on.

Steve's eyes went wide as he looked at the ring. Then he smiled and nodded. "I'd heard you'd gotten married. Not that it was all that surprising. I figured a woman like you wouldn't stay single for very long."

Rina shrugged. She didn't want to tell him she was single now, that her husband had passed away. Not to him, never to him. She had let him break her heart once before. There was no way she was going to let him do that again.

Even if he is single? A little voice in her head asked her. She dismissed that voice, though, not knowing for sure if he was single or not. She knew he had gotten a divorce from Avery's mother, but that didn't mean he was single. For all she knew, he was dating someone else or had even gotten married again.

But the way his eyes roamed over her, looking at her like she was the only person in the world.... He'd looked at her like that when they had been younger. That gaze had been enough to fool her into thinking she would be his forever.

Life didn't work that way, though—nor did teenage boys. And no matter what Rina did, she never could compare to Holly. So she really shouldn't have been surprised at all the times she had caught his gaze wandering to her whenever she'd been in the room.

Rina snorted. Back then, she'd blamed Holly. She'd blamed her older sister for the fact her boyfriend couldn't keep it in his pants. God, how stupid could she have been? She should have kicked him to the curb right then and there, rather than trying to impress him, rather than distancing herself from Holly.

"You guys know each other?" Avery asked, looking between the two of them like she'd just stepped into an alternate reality.

Rina forced a smile onto her face. This was one of the times when being able to put on a mask came in handy. "Oh, yes. We went to high school together. We're old friends," she said, putting her emphasis on old.

Steve chuckled as he put a hand on his daughter's shoulder, guiding her to sit in the seat she had vacated in her excitement a few moments ago. "Really, Avery. You should know by now everyone around here knows everyone."

Rina and Steve locked eyes again, and Rina shuddered. The locals all knew each other, just not quite to the extent how much they knew each other.

CHAPTER THIRTEEN

Rina wasn't sure what was more exhausting - her night out with the girls or trying to get through breakfast with Steve Trapper and his daughter. It took far more mental effort than Rina was used to in order for her to keep her focus on the wedding and not the man sitting directly across from her.

They had both been suitably impressed by the photos Rina showed them. She had chosen ones from some of the biggest and best weddings she'd done over the years, specifically chosen to display different aspects of the various days Rina had managed to wrangle into coming together perfectly.

And Rina's suspicion about almost everything already being planned out was correct. Avery had gotten all the contact information for the venue, the caterers, the musicians, and everyone else who had been contracted for her big day. Now, all Rina had to do was make sure everyone showed up on time and did the things they were supposed to do.

Just another day of wrangling cats, she mused as she put all the information into her tablet. The planning of a wedding was the tedious part. Making sure it all came together was the hard part. But it was nothing she hadn't done a million times and was more than up to the challenge.

Steve had insisted on paying for their breakfast, which Rina accepted graciously. The food had been delicious, though she'd been in work mode the majority of the time and hadn't quite had the chance to savor it as much as she would have liked.

But it was a business breakfast, after all. Which she was thoroughly glad about since it meant she could devote her attention primarily toward Avery and try to pretend Steve didn't exist.

As they stood to leave, Avery hugged Rina one final time, once again thanking her profusely. "I've gotta go meet up with my bridesmaids so they can try on their dresses, but please call me any time if you need anything. And if my mother somehow manages to get a hold of you, just hang up on her!"

Rina laughed and nodded. Something told her Avery was more than used to apologizing for her mother over the years. Part of her had wanted to know just who Steve Trapper had ended up marrying, but she wasn't sure she really wanted to know.

Speaking of the devil, she turned and locked eyes with him, nodding once. She was eager to get back to the house and start making calls to make sure everything was on schedule for the wedding. Oh, who was she kidding? She was eager to get back to the house and get as far away from Steve as she possibly could.

"Would you join me for a walk on the beach?" Steve asked, graciously enough Rina knew it would have been rude to refuse him. Because, of course, it was. The universe just really enjoyed tormenting her, didn't it? "I'd love to spend some time catching up with you if you think you can spare a few more minutes."

Minutes? Somehow, Rina doubted this trip down memory lane was only going to last a couple of minutes. She wanted to beg off to make excuses about having to get started on the wedding. But the look in his eyes said he knew as well as she did she could afford to spare the time to chat with him, which was how she ended up walking along the beach, side by side with the man she had sworn off so many years ago.

For a long while, neither of them said anything. They just walked along the edge of the ocean, taking in the view and making sure to keep at least a foot between each other. There'd been many days when they had walked hand and hand along these shores, but those days were long gone.

"Is Avery your only child?" Rina found herself asking, tired of the silence. If she was going to be stuck with the man, they might as well make small talk. Besides, her issues with Steve aside, Avery was a very sweet girl.

Steven nodded, looking almost sad at that. "Her mother and I were only married for two years before we split. Avery was just a baby at the time."

Rina nodded. From everything she had heard about this mystery woman, Rina wasn't surprised they hadn't been married for very long. Part of her wanted to rub it in his face, brag about the successful marriage she'd had. The other part of her felt guilty, which surprised her since this was the guy who had broken her heart.

"I've got two," Rina said, trying not to let her petty side take control. "Two boys."

Steve smirked as he nodded. "And let me guess, they're both handfuls, just like their mother?"

Rina snorted and then laughed before she shook her head. Oh, they were handfuls all right, but they weren't anything like her. They were much more level headed than she'd been. "They're good kids, though I guess they're not kids anymore. My youngest, Conner, just graduated. Trevor's twenty-one now."

God, it really was hard to believe just how much time had flown. Her babies really weren't babies anymore. She could still remember bringing them home from the hospital, feeding them, changing their diapers... It all still felt like it had just happened yesterday.

"They grow up fast, don't they?" Steve gave her a sad smile as he shook his head. "I swear it was just last week she was telling me boys were gross and had cooties, and now she's getting married. It's like, you blink and time just slips by you, huh?"

"That it does," Rina agreed.

The tension between them slipped away, little by little. Rina asked herself if she was really going to hold a grudge against him for something he had done as a kid. Wasn't she constantly chastising herself for having held a grudge against Holly for all these years?

Maybe it was time to let her grudge against Steve go, too.

The conversation flowed easier between the two of them, the longer they walked. Steve even told her about his ex-wife, all without Rina having to ask. "I can't believe I ever married her. She was always a nightmare. I guess it just took me a while to realize it. I'm just glad I did while Avery was still young. I had primary custody, thankfully, so she only had to put up with limited interaction with her mother."

"It must've been tough for her growing up. I guess we were lucky? We both had pretty good parents."

"Yeah, yeah, we did. I was sorry to hear about your father's passing. He was always a good man."

"Yeah, he was..." Rina let out a sigh, her gaze drifting out over the water. She watched as birds swooped down once in a while, trying their luck at catching a fish snack. When she was little, she had wished she could be a bird, to have the freedom to take to the skies and fly wherever she had wanted.

Now, she found herself reliving that childhood dream.

"You okay?" Steve asked, bringing her back to reality.

She looked at him and saw the concern in his eyes. How many times had he looked at her like that when they'd been together like he was willing to tackle whatever problems were ailing her?

Before she could stop herself, she told him the truth. "Dennis died about six months ago."

Steve froze in place. He stood there, slowly sinking into the sand, and stared at her with wide eyes. She waited for the look of pity that she had come to expect whenever she told someone her secret. But with Steve... no pity came. Just compassion and... sadness?

"God, Rina. I'm so sorry to hear that. I can't imagine how hard that must've been for you." He took a step forward, like he wanted to hug her, and then stopped himself. He let out a sigh and shook his head. "And here I am, rambling on about my ex-wife."

Rina shrugged. "Don't worry about it. Sometimes it's nice to know I'm not the only one who's had so much bad luck happen to them. It makes me feel a bit more... normal, you know?"

"Yeah, I get it," Steve smirked and shook his head again. "You always did have a unique way of looking at things! I guess that hasn't really changed, huh?"

"Some things just stay the same," Rina teased with a wink. Then, she laughed and started walking down the beach again, making Steve jog to catch up.

Maybe it really was time to move on.

CHAPTER FOURTEEN

The sun had just started to set, casting beautiful reds and oranges and pinks down onto the waves below it. Rina marveled at the sight, once again amazed at the breathtaking views from the island. She still couldn't believe she had given all of this up, that she had walked away and been okay with never coming back.

She really had been such an idiot back then. She just hoped it wasn't too late to make up for all of that.

"Join me for dinner?" Steve asked, his eyes twinkling. It wasn't until he'd asked the question that Rina realized just how long they had been out walking.

Their couple of minutes stroll had turned into an all-day affair, and now that food was mentioned, her stomach growled at the thought. She had skipped lunch, and even though she'd been positively stuffed after their late breakfast, that had been hours ago!

"Sure. That sounds nice," Rina said with a nod. Still, a part of her wanted to deny his request, but she found she actually enjoyed his company. Not that she should have been all that surprised. He had been charming when he was younger too. That much certainly hadn't changed.

He led her a bit farther down the shore, then up to the very edge of the sand, to a restaurant bustling with life. People mingled around on the back patio, where a small wooden bar was set up along with a handful of tall tables. When they headed around to the front, Rina was shocked at the line of people extending out into the parking lot.

She was about to suggest they headed somewhere less busy when Steve winked at her and pulled her inside before she could say anything. He walked over to the young woman at the hostess stand and whispered something to her. She nodded vigorously and then led them through the busy dining area to a small table in the back just big enough for the two of them.

Like a true gentleman, he slid Rina's chair out for her. Then, he winked at her again. "I'll be back in a moment, okay? Order yourself some wine or something when the waitress comes by. My treat!"

Again, Rina didn't have a chance to even open her mouth to respond. She expected to see him walk off in the direction of the bathrooms. They had been out walking along the beach for the better part of the day, after all. But instead, he made a beeline toward the kitchen, pushing the swinging double-wide doors open and disappearing inside.

A polite young woman came by the table a few minutes later, and Rina did indeed order herself a glass of red wine. Something told her if she was going to have dinner alone with Steven Trapper, she was going to need a bit of the liquid courage to keep her going.

She was actually on her second glass of wine when she started wondering where the man had gone. Had he slipped out the back, leaving Rina sitting alone and waiting for him? Was it some kind of childish prank he had decided to play on her?

A few minutes later, the kitchen doors flung open, and Rina turned, staring with her mouth hanging open as Steve wandered out into the dining area carrying two steaming hot plates in his hands. With all the flourish of an expert, he laid one in front of her and the other in front of his own seat.

"What?" was the only word Rina could form as she stared at the fresh cut of salmon laying over a bed of steaming pasta. She glanced around the restaurant, noticing a stark difference between the casual food of the rest of the diners compared to the near gourmet dish that had just been set in front of her.

Steve laughed as he slid into his own chair, pulling the plate closer toward him. He grinned at Rina's stunned expression, clearly amused at completely confusing her. "Guess you didn't know I had gone to culinary school after you left, huh?"

Rina shook her head. Honestly, when she had left Islamorada, Steve was probably the absolute last person on the planet she had wanted to think about. She'd had considerable resentment toward her siblings for various reasons, but none of that had compared to how she had felt about Steve.

"Yep, spent two years learning how to cook properly. I worked at a few restaurants on the varying islands before eventually settling down back here. I've been working here ever since, and when the old owner decided he wanted to retire and spend his days relaxing, I bought the place from him. I don't get to spend nearly as much time in the kitchen anymore, but being the owner has its benefits."

He waved his hands at the food in front of them. And, a couple of moments later, the waitress returned with glasses of wine for both of them. Rina glanced at her half-empty glass and then nodded her thanks to the woman.

She was going to need that third glass if things kept up like this!

Rina stared down at the food as her stomach rumbled again. Even though she was still shell shocked by this new revelation, her stomach was perfectly happy to remind her she still hadn't eaten since breakfast!

At least now she knew why the hostess hadn't given them menus!

She had never pictured Steve becoming a chef, but after her first bite, Rina knew it was his calling. The food was to die for, and she had to fight to keep herself from devouring every last bite in record time. And when she did finally finish it, she eyed the empty plate, wondering just what Steve would say if she started licking it.

It was only because she was afraid of what that might do to his ego that she refrained.

Dessert was not hand made by her former fling, but the Death by Chocolate cake was very nearly as good as the pasta had been!

They sat and talked for a while, watching as the sunset over the water. It didn't take long before the beautiful colors were gone, revealing a sky dotted with twinkling stars.

"Are you excited about Avery's wedding this weekend?" Rina asked, glancing over at Steve

He let out a short bark of laughter and then gave her a sad smile. "Terrified, actually—after my marriage to her mother... Well,

I guess I just hope she doesn't end up making the same mistakes I did, you know?"

"Oh, don't worry. If she's anything like mine, she's far too smart to make the same mistakes." Rina smiled sadly as she shook her head. She had worried about the same thing for years, but time after time, her boys proved to have a bit more sense in their heads than she'd had. Not that they didn't make their own mistakes, of course, but at least she didn't have to sit and watch history repeat itself with them!

"God, I love Avery to death, but sometimes I wish I had boys," Steve smirked and then laughed. "Girls are so... I don't even know how to describe it, but I swear just watching her leave the house has me biting my nails, praying for her to be okay, you know?"

"It's not much different with the boys. I still worry about them, even if they do just roll their eyes." Rina shrugged. "But it's what parents do. We worry, no matter what gender the kids are."

Rina couldn't believe how easy it was to talk to Steve. After all the years of resentment, after spending so much time crying in her room because he had broken her heart, she'd thought those days of sitting and talking and laughing with him were far behind her.

And yet, there she was, sitting in the restaurant he owned, just talking like they were old friends.

Steve, ever the gentleman, drove her back to the Inn after they finally finished dinner. When they pulled up in front of the house, she almost didn't want to get out of the car. She didn't want the night to end.

God, what had she gotten herself into?

CHAPTER FIFTEEN

GIDDY. RINA WAS GIDDY! SHE GRINNED EVEN AS SHE SHOOK her head, slowly making her way up the dirt path leading to the house. She really did feel like a schoolgirl again, pining over the one boy on the island she couldn't have.

Except... what was stopping her from having him now? Obviously, he had gotten over his thing for Holly unless he had somehow been too late before Jake had snapped her back up.

Maybe she was getting in over her head, letting her emotions and instincts guide her down a path that was only going to lead to more heartache and pain. But she wasn't sure what other choice she had. It wasn't like she could control her feelings toward him. Nor could she just avoid him and pretend he didn't exist.

She'd committed to helping Avery make sure her wedding went off without a hitch. It was too late to back out now, not that she really wanted to. Avery was a sweet girl, and she wasn't going to risk ruining her big day just because she couldn't stop pining over the girl's father.

She would have to figure something out, though, before she ended up making a mistake, she would no doubt regret down the road.

But that was a problem for tomorrow, she decided. There was no sense in worrying about it tonight. It wasn't like she was planning on sneaking out and stealing the family boat just to spend some time with him. She may have felt like a teenager again, but she most certainly wasn't sixteen anymore!

Rina glanced in the direction of the boathouse, but it was silent tonight. None of Randy's employees were picking up miss-delivered packages this time. The area around the Archer House was nearly silent except for the sounds of the waves crashing against the shore and the occasional cricket chirping away.

When she walked inside, though, that was a whole different story. Laughter came from the kitchen, which made Rina raise an eyebrow. This late at night, she figured everyone would be getting ready for bed. Or, if not, then at least being quiet for those who were.

But when she followed the sound of laughter, she found not only Holly and their mother still awake at the table, with magazines scattered in front of them, but Holly's daughter Gabby was there as well. Everyone looked up when she walked in, grinning at her.

"Aunt Rina!" Gabby exclaimed, hopping up from the table. She rushed over to hug her aunt, and Rina hugged her back. They had never been particularly close since Rina had avoided Holly as much as the rest of her siblings, but now that that was in the past, it was well overdue for her to spend a bit of quality time with her niece!

"It's so good to see you, Gabby! How are you? Holly told me you're expecting? Congratulations!" If Rina wasn't destined to have a daughter, at the very least, she could gush over her niece. That was how that worked.

"I'm doing good. We were just looking at bridal magazines so I can get an idea of what I want for my wedding. Wanna join us?"

"Oh, honey, you just said the magic words!" Rina grinned broadly. An excuse to pour over bridal magazines? Yes, please! Sign her right up!

Rina sat down in one of the empty chairs while Gabby pointed out the various things she liked and didn't like from the magazines. The girl talked a mile a minute and Rina had to struggle to keep up with everything she said. Nelly and Holly just sat there smirking, clearly enjoying being able to sit and watch someone else suffer through Gabby's pre-wedding excitement.

"You know you're not going to be able to have everything, right?" Holly teased, gently elbowing her daughter. She was smiling, though, clearly happy about the idea of her daughter tying the knot in the near future.

Gabby sighed and shook her head. "I know, I know. It's just so hard to choose! And like, what if it looks good in the magazine, but when I see it in real life, it's hideous?"

Rina had to fight back her laughter. She'd seen so many brides-to-be in the same boat, anxious over making the right choices. Most of them had been dreaming about their weddings since they were little girls, so everything had to be just perfect.

"Would it help to see a wedding first hand?" Rina offered, and when Gabby's eyes lit up, Rina actually did chuckle. "Well, I agreed to help a girl with her wedding this weekend. Her wedding planner bailed at the last minute, so I stepped in to help her out. You're welcome to come with me if you want. You can be my helper or something and see what things you actually like and don't like."

"Oh. My. God. Yes, please! Can I really?" Gabby was literally bouncing up and down in her chair. Looking at her, you would have thought she was still seven, not twenty-six!

But hey, at least it would give her a chance to spend some time with her niece. She'd missed out on years of bonding with her, so it would be nice for them to hang out together, just the two of them.

It wouldn't replace the daughter she had always wanted, but it might just quench that dream a bit.

CHAPTER SIXTEEN

RINA DID A SURVEY OF THE CHAIRS AND TABLES STACKED UP IN the large room the Inn used for conferences or indoor events. Holly had made sure there weren't any other events scheduled at the Inn for the weekend, which meant they had full access to all of the resources the Inn had on hand. If Rina had been planning the event, she'd have already started setting the tables and chairs out, planning where they'd all go. But since Holly was still adamant the party was to be a surprise, Rina was stuck mapping it all out mentally.

"Think we've got enough space for everyone?" Randy asked, making Rina jump. She had been so lost in thought she hadn't heard him walk up.

Pursing her lips, Rina thought about it for a moment and then nodded. Since it would be an informal event, they wouldn't need chairs for every single person. She highly doubted everyone would be trying to sit down at the same time like they would at a wedding or conference. Plus, she doubted everyone would even all be there at the same time. So long as she had enough seats for the majority of the attendees, she figured they would be fine.

"I wish Holly wasn't so set on this being a surprise party. It makes it that much harder to plan everything."

Randy laughed and then shrugged before patting his sister on the back. "Yeah, well. You know Holly. Once she's got her mind set on something, there's not much that can change it."

Rina let out a sigh and then nodded. Randy wasn't wrong. If there was one person in the world more stubborn than Rina, it was her older sister, which was probably the biggest reason they had stopped getting along as they grew up.

The sister in question was with her daughter, going over the decorations for the party. It was so strange to basically be a glorified helper monkey when she was so used to being the one coordinating everything. Even if she hadn't done any event planning in a couple of months, it really was like riding a bike. More than once, she'd had to bite her tongue and let Holly take the lead. This party was her idea, after all, and Rina didn't want to upset her by trying to take it over.

She hadn't come back to town just to steal Holly's thunder.

Knocking on the event hall's door made both Rina and Randy turn, the sister in question standing in the doorway. Holly grinned at both of them, clearly pleased at how the party was all coming together which, Rina figured was a good thing. At least she wasn't one of those obsessive planners where nothing was ever good enough.

"I'm getting ready to head out and pick up the cake. Does either of you want to come with me? Gabby's going to hang out here and take a break." Holly smirked and then let out a short laugh. "Though I'm pretty sure she's going to spend the entire time flipping through those bridal magazines. She's definitely got wedding fever!"

Rina laughed and nodded. They had been up late the other night, talking about all the different options for a wedding. And if Rina didn't know any better, she'd swear Gabby was more excited for tomorrow's wedding than the actual bride!

"Sure, I'll go with you. If I have to sit here staring at tables, trying to decide just how to lay them out on Sunday any longer, I think I'm gonna tear my hair out." If she had been allowed to drag everything outside and actually set it all up, she would have been done relatively quickly. But since she had to do it all mentally, it really was driving her nuts. She didn't want the tables too close together, but nor did she want them all just scattered around.

"I think I'll hang out here. A break does sound good right about now..." Randy said with a smirk, earning himself a smack in the arm from Rina. "What? I don't know crap about planning a party and you both know that! I'll earn my keep on Sunday when I'm the one carting all these tables and chairs outside!"

Rina couldn't really argue with him. She fully planned on taking advantage of having his muscle on hand. Sure, she could carry all the stuff outside and set it up herself, but it would be much easier to have someone do all the heavy lifting while she looked at the bigger picture and made sure everything was laid out just right.

Plus, it would be fun to make Randy sweat a bit. What was the point of having a little brother if you couldn't boss him around and make him do all the hard work?

So while he and Gabby lounged around, Rina and Holly

headed toward the bakery to pick up the cake. "So, where are you planning on keeping this cake so that Mom won't find it?" Rina asked eyebrow raised. With how paranoid Holly was about not letting their mom in on the secret, she figured Holly wouldn't want to pick up the cake until Sunday morning.

But, of course, Holly had a solution for that. Because why wouldn't Miss Perfect have thought of everything? "Chef Stevens agreed to store them in the kitchen's walk-in fridge. Mom never went in there even when she was taking an active role in the Inn. No way is she going to just randomly decide to go for a stroll in there."

Rina had to admit, that was a good plan. As much as she hated her sister always being perfect, she couldn't complain with her results.

Holly let out a sigh and ran a hand through her hair. Rina frowned, looking her sister over. Holly looked more stressed than usual. "What's up?" Rina asked. Was she still recuperating from the stress of her ex? Or because of Mom's health still not being the greatest? "You looked stressed."

"I still can't figure out where the Inn's money is going," Holly said, letting out another sigh. Her grip on the steering wheel tightened until her knuckles turned white. "We're booked solid almost every week. There's no reason the business accounts shouldn't be overflowing with how few repairs have been done over the last several years. Uncle Roger and I have gone over the accounting together, but it still doesn't make sense. And every time I ask Mom, she just gives me vague answers and changes the subject."

Rina nodded. She could understand how that would be

stressful. And if Holly couldn't get to the bottom of the problem, there was a very good chance the Inn would go right back downhill once she left. Then Mom would be right back where she'd started, and no doubt her health would backpedal as well.

"Well, if I've got some time before I head back, I'll look over it all with you. Maybe some fresh eyes will help spot where the money is going."

Holly nodded, giving Rina an appreciative smile. Then, she let out a short laugh. "The only problem is getting you to have some free time! Between Mom's party on Sunday and the wedding tomorrow, you're going to be a busy little bee this weekend!"

"Ugh, don't remind me!" Rina let out a laugh of her own. "I don't mind doing the wedding. I could practically do it in my sleep at this point. And Avery is a sweet girl. She's nothing like some of the Bridezillas I've dealt with in the past. I just wish she didn't have to be Steve Trapper's daughter! Of all the people on the island, I had to volunteer to help out."

This time, when Holly laughed, it was a loud, cackling sound that filled the interior of her Jag. She was enjoying Rina's predicament far too much, and Rina gave her a sour look. Just because Holly had decided to get back with her high school fling didn't mean Rina had any intentions of doing the same thing.

She wasn't going to keep holding a grudge against Steve, but she wasn't going to completely forgive him either. He had broken her heart once and no way was she going to give him the chance to do it again.

And yet, that didn't stop her heart from skipping a beat every time she thought about him—which just made her hate herself even more. Not only was this the guy who'd broken her heart, but it was also only six months after her husband had died.

She had no right feeling this way about anyone, much less Steve. God, what would Dennis say if he could see her now, having a school-girl crush on a guy only months after losing her husband of twenty-four years. She and Dennis had been married longer than she had live in Islamorada! It should've been a lot longer than six months before she was even ready to look at another guy, much less be falling for one!

"You know, Dennis isn't coming back. And I doubt he would want you to spend the rest of your life as a widow, becoming a crazy cat lady." Holly smirked at her, and Rina let out a sigh. Of course, Holly would know exactly what was going through her mind. God, even after almost thirty years apart, Holly could still read her like an open book. Even when they'd been angst-filled teenager, constantly at odds with each other, Holly had always seemed to know how Rina really felt, no matter how hard she tried to mask her feelings.

It had driven her nuts back then, and it certainly drove her nuts now! Even more so because Holly was right. Deep down, the logical part of her brain knew that. But darn if the rest of her didn't want to think about things logically.

"Being alone for the rest of my life and falling for a guy after six months are two different things, though. I mean, come on. Dennis and I were married for more than half of my life! A week ago, I would have told you I'd never be able to move on after him. And now here I am, swooning over a guy who already broke my heart once!"

Holly laughed and then reached over to squeeze Rina's

shoulder. "No one ever said love was easy. But you know, it is possible to feel two things at once. You can fall for someone new and still mourn your husband. And he broke your heart when you guys were kids. Don't you think he's grown up a little bit since then?"

"Even if he has, what am I supposed to do, just give up my life in Naples and move back here? I've got a business back there! And I mean, yeah, the kids are leaving for college soon, so they don't exactly need me there, but still... My entire life is there."

"Your entire life used to be here," Holly pointed out. "That didn't stop you from picking up and leaving practically the day you turned eighteen, now did it? And this is just as big of a wedding destination as Naples. You could start a second location here and do just fine. Between that and birthdays, corporate conferences, and baby showers, you should be more than set."

Rina frowned again, even as she nodded. Once again, Holly had made a lot of sense. She could open up a second location here. Taking six months off had shown her staff was more than capable of running the business in Naples without her. And like she had said, the boys would be off starting the next chapter in their own lives, so she wouldn't even have them to tie her down anymore.

Maybe moving back to Islamorada wasn't such a far-fetched idea after all...

Rina couldn't help but laugh. She had spent years counting down the days until she could leave the islands behind and for even longer after that, she'd refused to even come back to visit unless she had been forced to. And now, there she was, sitting in the passenger seat of Holly's Jag, actually entertaining the idea of moving back to her childhood hometown.

Maybe the world really was coming to an end...

"MAYBE WE SHOULD'VE BORROWED RANDY'S TRUCK," RINA SAID with wide-eyed as she watched the baker and the young woman he had as an assistant bring out cake after cake. Just how many had Holly ordered? And how in the world did she expect to fit all of those in her tiny Jag?

Jeez, at this rate, they were going to end up tying them to the roof!

But, somehow, they managed to get them all in there. Holly should have entered a Tetris competition because Rina couldn't even fathom how she had managed to fit that many cakes in such a small space without ruining them all.

The entire drive back to the Inn, Rina had a white-knuckled grip on the car door. She kept waiting for Holly to take a turn too sharp or hit a pothole and send a cascade of frosting everywhere. Not only would it be a waste of delicious cake, but Rina was not looking forward to trying to scrub frosting out of Holly's car.

Though, if she was being honest, Holly would kinda deserve it for ordering as many as she had and not bringing a bigger car to pick them up! Or, more logically speaking, she could have had the baker deliver them! At least he had a nice big cargo van that would've easily fit this mountain of confection.

Somehow they managed to make it back to the Inn without incident, though Rina wasn't sure how they had managed it. Had they just used a year's worth of good luck on that trip? Because it certainly felt like it!

By the time they'd gotten everything loaded into the restaurant's fridge, Rina was fully exhausted. Who knew moving cake after cake could be such a workout? It had been so long since she'd had to do that herself, she'd forgotten. Maybe she was getting complacent, always relying on caterers or other help to handle all the heavy lifting.

Once it was all settled and tucked away in the back corner of the fridge, Rina went for a walk along the beach to relax. She still needed to go over the last-minute details of the wedding and make absolutely sure everything was in place for tomorrow, but she wanted a break to clear her mind for a little while.

It wouldn't do for her to be too mentally tired when she went over everything; otherwise, she was liable to make a mistake. And when it came to someone's wedding, she couldn't afford to make a mistake. A birthday or corporate event had a bit of leniency and flexibility to them. A wedding, though? Not a chance. That had to be completely perfect.

As she neared the boathouse, she noticed a familiar boat tethered to the end of the dock again. Rina frowned as she walked closer, Randy's friend giving her a sad wave as she did. Had Randy really screwed up again, ordering more stuff to the Inn by accident? Or was it all part of the same order and he hadn't gone in and changed the address to be the proper one? Either way was possible.

But then, why hadn't he grabbed the stuff himself when he'd been there earlier? Wouldn't that have been easier than sending one of his workers to get them? He hadn't seemed bad when she'd seen him earlier, but he could've just been better at hiding it these days. Either way, Rina was going to have to sit down and talk with her brother. If his alcoholism really was getting this bad, she couldn't just sit by and do nothing.

She stood there and watched the boat take off through the water, making a solid wake behind it. She made a mental note to talk to Holly about everything. If this had been going on for a while, then it was likely Holly had noticed as well. And maybe, if they worked together, they could find a way to talk some sense into their brother.

CHAPTER SEVENTEEN

GABBY YAWNED, LEANING BACK IN THE PASSENGER SEAT AND closing her eyes. Rina smirked and let out a soft chuckle. The sun had only just begun to peak over the horizon, so it was no wonder her niece was still half asleep. But if there was one thing Rina had learned in all her years of being an event planner, it was to be as early as possible when it came to a wedding.

She was herding cats, after all. And if she wasn't ready and willing to crack the whip, every last one of them would drag their feet. And even though she was doing this job for free, she was still going to make sure it was all done properly and the wedding went off without a hitch!

Especially if she really wanted to open up an event planning business there on that part of the island.

To her pleasure, the decorators were already on scene when she pulled up. A makeshift alter had already been erected on the beach, a good-sized area having been roped off for the wedding. A pair of teenage boys were busy setting up rows of chairs for the guests. And to their credit, they looked much more awake than Rina's so-called helper.

Rina nudged Gabby, still smirking, as they headed down the sandy beach toward the setup area. "Maybe we should've brought a second cup of coffee along for you!" Rina teased. Once she was sure things were going smoothly, she would slip off to a nearby cafe and pick some up for the both of them, but until then, they would have to push forward with just the cups they'd had from the house.

"Do you always get up this early for your weddings?" Gabby asked, stifling a yawn. Gabby had somehow found the energy to do her hair and makeup that morning, but even then, she still looked like the walking dead. The poor girl was definitely not a morning person.

That was one thing she hadn't inherited from her mother, it seemed!

Rina nodded. "I've learned that if I'm not here early, things tend not to get done. At least this way, if someone's not there or is slacking off, I can get it taken care of before it's too late. The sooner I can spot any problems, the sooner I can fix them before the bride notices. Because no matter how much people say a wedding is for both the bride and groom, I've learned it's almost always the brides who want everything picture perfect!"

Gabby giggled and nodded. The slight look of guilt in her eyes told Rina she was one of those brides. She just hoped her niece could rein it in enough to keep from turning into a monster bride.

Rina went to work, tracking down the various people who had been contracted to make Avery's dream come true. To her pleasant surprise, everyone was on the ball that morning, and as long as it stayed that way, things would go off without a hitch.

She shouldn't have been surprised, though. Back in Naples, she had dozens of caterers, decorators, and bridal shops she could choose from at any given time. Here in the Keys, there was only be a handful for her to choose from. If one of them slacked off or delivered subpar quality, word would spread like wildfire and they would be out of business quicker than they could blink.

That was certainly a welcomed change from the normal. And it definitely made it all the more tempting to open an event planning business there. The fewer headaches she had to deal with for each event, the better!

Once that was taken care of, Rina upheld her promise and took Gabby to get a cup of coffee. She may not have looked it, but Rina was just as tired as she was. A good, strong cup of coffee was just what she needed to be able to tackle the day at full strength.

By the time they made it back, the wedding party had started to arrive. Rina spotted Avery over with the baker, no doubt making sure her cake had arrived in one piece. Rina smirked and shook her head. No matter how many times she assured the brides to be that everything was going just fine, they still worried. Not that she could really blame them. She knew just how nervous they were. After all, she'd been in their shoes once before. And even though it had been many years ago, Rina distinctly remembered how she'd felt in the days leading up to her wedding.

"What do you think?" Rina asked Gabby, looking at the altar that was in the middle of being decorated. "Is there a beach wedding in your future? Or are you thinking something more traditional?"

Gabby pursed her lips and then shrugged. "I mean, I guess I always imagined a traditional wedding in a church, you know? But I kind of like the idea of getting married on the beach under the sun. There's just something... magical about it, you know?"

Rina nodded. Beach weddings were popular for a reason. Especially destination ones like Naples and Islamorada. For every wedding she had done for someone local to Naples, she probably handled at least two for brides and grooms that lived somewhere else and just wanted a slice of paradise for their big day.

"What about your husband? Does he have any preference? It's his big day, too, isn't it?"

Gabby laughed, the sound echoing around her. She grinned at Rina, a wide smile she wouldn't have been capable of pre-caffeine. "God, if he had his way, we would just pack our bags, hop on a plane to Vegas, and elope! He's a sweet man, but big fancy events aren't exactly his thing. As long as we end up married at the end of the day, he doesn't much care how it happens."

"Typical man."

"And who exactly are the two of you?" A screeching voice made Rina and Gabby both pause mid-conversation. Brow furrowed, Rina looked around for the source. Rina expected to see one of the contractors being berated. Instead, a bleach-blonde demon spitting hellfire was marching toward the pair of them. "This is a wedding, you know! You can't just march around here getting in the way!"

Rina stood there, one hand on her hip, eyebrow raised, and stared at the woman. She didn't need an introduction to know this was the famed mother who had scared off the last wedding planner. Luckily for Avery, Rina wasn't so easily scared off. While Gabby took a step back and looked ready to bolt, Rina just continued to stare at the woman, not even blinking.

"What, are you just going to stand there and ignore me? I should call the cops and have you arrested for trespassing!" The woman was only a couple feet away now, looking angrier each second Rina ignored her questions.

"Jennifer!" A booming voice interrupted the woman's tirade. Both her and Rina turned to see Steve marching toward them; a deep frown etched onto his face. No doubt, Avery had tasked her father with reining in her mother, and the brief interaction they'd had made Rina wonder how Steve didn't have more gray in his hair. "That's Rina Renner, the woman who so kindly stepped up at the last moment after you ran off the last wedding planner?"

Rina had to fight back her laughter at the woman's shocked expression. She looked back and forth between Rina and Steve; her expression souring each moment. She opened her mouth, no doubt to say something else scathing, but Steve cut her off.

"You're the mother of the bride, remember? Isn't it your job to be with her, keeping her calm? I think Rina has everything here under control. Why don't you go take care of Avery." Steve waited until Jennifer let out a sigh and nodded before winking at Rina and slipping off in the direction of the caterers.

Rina watched as Jennifer stood and watched her ex-husband walk away, her lips pursed like she'd just sucked on a lemon. Rina couldn't for the life of her figure out what Steve had seen in this woman, but it really wasn't any of his business.

She pulled her purse around and then rummaged around inside it before pulling out a flask and taking a long drink of it. "He never was my type," the woman muttered as she continued to stare at Steve's back. "I just wanted a kid, and he was good looking enough to settle as the donor."

Rina kept her mouth shut, and the woman wandered off a minute later. She watched her go, giving her the same sour look she'd given Steve. God, Steve must have been out of his mind to ever marry that woman. It was a wonder him and Avery had managed to stay sane after having to deal with her regularly.

"That was the bride's mother?" Gabby asked incredulously. She frowned and then shook her head. "God, and here I thought Mom was a handful sometimes!"

Rina laughed and nodded. As much as Holly drove her nuts, she wasn't even close to as bad as that woman. And while she had no doubt Holly would be almost as nervous as Gabby when the big day finally came around, she knew her sister would at least be able to control herself better than that.

With Momzilla out of the way, Avery and Gabby were free to continue checking how everything was going. She was more than a little pleased at just how smoothly things were going along. Even with the monster of a mother, Rina couldn't figure out why the wedding planner would've backed out that close to the wedding. By that point, everything was basically finished!

Gabby wanted to get another cup of coffee before the wedding actually started, so while she did that, Rina went in search of Steve. Even though she hadn't really needed his help with Jennifer, she still appreciated it.

She found him and the chef laughing together. No doubt, the two of them knew each other. The island wasn't nearly big enough for the various chefs not to have interacted a good bit over the years.

When he saw her walking over, though, Steve said something to the chef and then headed in her direction.

"Jennifer's not still throwing tantrums for no reason, is she?" Steve teased with a smirk.

"No, not this time. I just wanted to thank you for stepping in. Not that you had to, of course. She wasn't the first touchy mother I've had to deal with over the years."

"Yeah, I can imagine having to deal with weddings. You're more than used to having your head bitten off by now. But then, you never did let much get to you, did you?"

Other than you? Rina thought to herself. Steve had always been the one person who had been able to get under her skin. Well, other than her siblings, of course, but Rina didn't count them. Family always knew just how to press your buttons, didn't they?

"How're you holding up? Still worried about Avery?"

Steve gave her a half-smile, then shrugged. He tried to act nonchalant about it, but Rina saw right through his weak attempt. Apparently, she still knew him pretty well, despite their years apart.

"You really don't have to, you know? Avery's a good girl. She's got a good head on her shoulders. She's not going to make the same mistake you did."

Steve let out a sigh and then nodded. His shoulder slumped slightly, and Rina could tell he wanted to agree with her, but his nerves just wouldn't let him. She understood that completely. The logical part of his brain wasn't always the one in control. "Thanks, Rina," he said, though, looking into her eyes.

Rina's heart skipped a beat as she stared back. Her mouth went dry as she struggled to look away, but something about the way

Steve looked her had her mesmerized. She couldn't look anywhere else. Part of her didn't even want to.

Part of her wanted to step even closer to him.

Wanted to kiss him.

That thought snapped Rina out of her daze. She was not going to kiss Steve. It was not going to happen, no matter how badly that illogical part of her mind screamed at her to do exactly that.

"Well, it's going to be time for you to walk your daughter down the aisle soon. So I should let you go prepare. I'll see you later!" Rina said quickly before turning and hurrying away from the man who once again had found a way under her skin.

CHAPTER EIGHTEEN

"I NOW PRONOUNCE YOU HUSBAND AND WIFE!" THE MINISTER'S booming voice echoed across the crowd. Even from far back, Rina could hear him clearly. "You may now kiss the bride!"

The audience erupted into applause as Avery was swept off her feet and given the kiss of a lifetime. Even Rina found herself clapping, glad she had gotten to give the girl the special day she'd wanted. How the other wedding planner could just bail at the last minute like that, potentially ruining her big day, was beyond Rina. She'd have never done something like that to one of her clients. If she was going to quit, she made sure to do it well in advance of whatever event it was. At least that would give the client a chance to find someone else to fill her shoes.

Sniffling caught Rina's attention, and she glanced over at Gabby just in time to see the young woman wiping tears from her eyes. Rina smirked and chuckled to herself. Gabby didn't even know these people, and there she was, getting all worked up.

But then, that was the magical effect of a wedding. Even if you didn't know the people, there was just something in the air at a wedding that made you happy and excited for the couple. Rina just couldn't imagine not brimming with enthusiasm at something like this.

Maybe that was why she had always preferred to do weddings over other kinds of events. Sure, they were much more stressful, but the pay off at the end was so much more satisfying. Nothing made her feel like she had done a good job like the broad grins on a bride and groom's face as they walked back down the aisle together, hand in hand, ready to start the next chapter in their lives.

Once the couple had slipped off to get some photos done with their family, Rina nudged Gabby and motioned toward the large area of circular tables with long buffets aligned around them. "Come on. I've gotta make sure everything's good to go for the reception," Rina whispered.

Gabby nodded and followed her. Not that Rina really needed her to, but she still liked the enthusiasm Gabby had shown all day. Even though Rina knew she'd really only been there to watch and get ideas for her own wedding, she had been eager to help with anything Rina needed.

The caterer was indeed ready to go. All the food was spread out beautifully, and helpers were in the middle of uncovering it all when Rina walked over. The two minibars that had been set up were staffed and smiling from ear to ear, their empty tip jars sending off glittering sparkles as the high Florida sun shone down on them. By the end of the day, they'd no doubt be stuffed to the brim.

Just as Rina finished her rounds, people began flooding over to the area. The wedding wasn't the biggest one Rina had ever managed, but there was still a good number of people there to celebrate with the happy bride and groom, and all of them looked ravenous!

The sound of the band filled the area as people mingled around, laughing and joking as they filled plates high with various types of food. Rina mingled as well, talking with the guests she knew and listening to what people thought about the wedding.

Everyone had good things to say, and Rina beamed with pride. Even though she had only taken over at the last minute, it still felt good to hear people telling her how amazing everything was.

Eventually, the bride and groom returned, wearing much more comfortable clothes. People swarmed them, everyone looking to offer their congratulations. Rina walked over to the bar area, avoiding the mob, not wanting to get caught in the stampede. She would have plenty of time to talk to the lucky couple later before they disappeared on their honeymoon.

Rina felt like she had been floating on cloud nine as she bounced around the reception, checking and double-checking that no problems had popped up. For the first time in six months, she felt normal. Maybe taking so much time off work to grieve hadn't been such a great idea. Maybe she should have gone back to work sooner, gotten herself back into a normal routine.

She was glad she'd listened to her instincts and volunteered to take over the wedding at the last minute. Even though it had been a bit more stress than she'd planned on for her little trip, she couldn't deny just how much it took her mind off everything.

Steve sidled up to her, giving her a wide smile. Rina could smell the alcohol on his breath, and she wondered just how many cocktails he had treated himself to already. His speech wasn't slurred, though, nor did he look like he was swaying even a little, so she figured it hadn't been too many. "Guess it's too late to object now, huh?" he teased, making Rina laugh.

"Well, I guess you can technically object at any time. I'm just not sure the bride and groom would appreciate it, though." Rina winked at Steve and then elbowed him gently. "Besides, look at how happy they are. Would you really want to be the one to rain on their parade?"

"No, no, I guess I wouldn't. I'm not sure Avery would ever forgive me if I ruined her special moment. Guess I'll just have to suffer in silence over my baby girl being all grown up."

Rina giggled and elbowed him again. He had such a knack for drama, but it still made her laugh. But even talking to Steve wasn't enough to ruin her good mood. She had worked hard for this, and she was glad it'd all turned out perfectly.

Nothing was going to get her down today!

CHAPTER NINETEEN

"I think you need a drink!" Steve declared, grinning again. "And I think I need one too!"

"You can go ahead, but I'm technically working. I'm not sure Avery would appreciate her wedding planner getting drunk at the wedding! Nor would your ex-wife, I'm sure. Wouldn't want to give her any more ammunition, would we?"

Steve pouted. He honest to God stood there and pouted at her like he was a toddler who'd just been told he couldn't have ice cream before bed. "You're just no fun, are you?"

"Oh, stop being a drama queen. That's the bride's job." Rina rolled her eyes and shook her head. Speaking of the bride.... She scanned the crowd, but it wasn't too hard to find the grinning woman as she danced barefoot in the sand with her husband.

A young woman walked by, blocking her view. Rina blinked a few times, looking at the girl in a caterer's outfit, holding a silver tray of cream puffs. She looked back at Rina and just stood there.

Rina frowned and raised an eyebrow, but the girl still didn't say anything.

"Shouldn't you be circling?" Rina asked, nodding toward the tray of cream puffs. She hadn't even actually offered them to her or Steve. She just stood there staring at Rina like she had an extra head or something.

The girl jumped a bit, her eyes going wide. She let out a startled squeak, then nodded and quickly scurried off. Rina watched her until she disappeared into the crowd, still frowning.

What in the world had that been about? she wondered to herself.

Everything had gone perfectly so far, so she wasn't about to get her panties in a knot because of a single strange server. If that was the biggest problem she had today, then she was going to consider herself very lucky.

"You know her?" Steve asked. His gaze in the direction the girl had disappeared.

Rina shook her head, then shrugged. "No, but then I don't really know any of the catering staff here. And she's far too young for me to have known her when I lived here. She barely looks like she's my youngest son's age!"

Steve nodded, but his gaze was still on the crowd. Then, he let out a sigh and shrugged. "Guess that's probably not even the weirdest thing you've seen at a wedding."

"Oh, God, not even close." Rina laughed, the memory already playing in her mind. "There was this one where the bride insisted on everyone wearing neon colors instead of traditional white and black. Like, I know some brides want their bridesmaids to be in bright and vibrant colors, but this woman wanted everyone wearing neon. Even her wedding dress was bright pink. The poor girl looked like a walking highlight as she came down the aisle!"

Steve burst out laughing, his deep voice echoing even over the noise of the crowd. The sound sent shivers through Rina's body, and she had to fight the urge to inch closer to him, to lean against him and have him put his arm around her.

God, she really needed to get herself under control! She was at his daughter's wedding for crying out loud. This was not the time to be having those kinds of thoughts about him.

A loud squeak followed by a grunt and a clattered sound caught Rina's attention. She let out a sigh and then gave Steve a shrug and a sad smile before heading off in the direction of the commotion. She pushed through the crowd just in time to see a man in a suit helping the server from earlier stand again.

Her tray was on the sand, along with most of the cream puffs. The remaining ones were squished against the front of her uniform. Rina let out another sigh. The poor girl looked ready to burst into tears. Before Rina could even call for someone to come help clean up, two servers were already rushing over to start cleaning up the scattered food.

Rina nodded, a pleased smile on her face. She really did enjoy working with professionals. It didn't get much better than having people who knew what to do before Rina could even ask for it. She walked over and apologized to the man, then quickly whisked the server away from the scene of the accident before she could have a complete meltdown.

"Relax," Rina told the girl, doing her best to keep her voice calm and collected. An accident like that was easily fixable and forgotten. The girl was the one who'd ended up covered in the cream puffs, rather than the guest, so she doubted he would kick up much of a stink.

At least it hadn't been Avery's mother she had bumped into. If that had happened, Rina was pretty sure she would never have lived it down.

"Accidents happen, okay? The others probably have it all cleaned up by now and the guests have gone back to celebrating." The girl blinked at Rina through her tears, so Rina grinned at her. "The only real casualty is your uniform. You're gonna have some scrubbing to do tonight."

The girl sniffled and nodded. She'd started to calm down, but as Rina watched her keep glancing back in the direction of the party, she could tell the girl was only moments away from backsliding into waterworks.

"It happens to all of us. My first wedding, I wasn't looking where I was going and bumped into the maid of honor. She was wearing these really thin flats and I ended up stepping on her foot and breaking her big toe. She had to walk with a limp for the rest of the wedding."

The girl looked at her with wide-eyes and completely horror-stricken at the thought. Rina laughed and nodded, remembering that day clear as ever. She had freaked out after that, sure that her career working weddings were in the toilet. But the woman had been gracious enough not to flip out, and now Rina could laugh about the whole thing.

It had certainly made her first wedding memorable!

"Thanks," the girl said, nodding and wiping the tears away.

"What's your name?" Rina asked.

"Beth... And I'm really sorry about bumping into that guy. It's just... this is my first wedding. And I guess I got distracted..."

"It happens to the best of us. Don't worry too much about it, okay? Just take some time, get a drink of water, and see if you can clean some of that cream puff off your uniform."

The girl looked down at the splattered remains of the cream puffs and made a sour face. Then, she giggled and looked at Rina and nodded. "There should be spare uniforms in the truck. I'll go change into one."

"Perfect." Rina patted the girl on the back. That was one crisis averted. Thankfully it had been an easy one, and as the girl went to walk off, Rina let out a sigh. If only all of her weddings went this smoothly.

The girl walked a few feet away, then paused and turned around. She pursed her lips as she looked Rina up and down like she was appraising an antique. "You know, you don't really seem like the evil person my mom said you were. I mean, I still don't get why you won't give me my inheritance, but I don't think it's because you're a bad person."

Rina stood there, mouth gaping open, as the girl shrugged and walked off like what she said was totally normal. A thousand questions shot through her mind, overloading it until she couldn't even form a single word. She was left standing there like a loon, trying to figure out what in the world had just happened.

Why couldn't her life just be simple?

CHAPTER TWENTY

By the time she came back to her senses, the girl was gone. She wandered back to the party, heart racing, as she kept an eye out for Debbie. She should have known something was going on the moment that girl had stopped and stared at her like that. But she had been so lost in her own satisfaction that she had ignored the weird tingle that had gone through her.

She had to force a smile onto her face as family members wandered over to tell her what a beautiful wedding it had been. It really was a good thing she'd done a thousand of these. That meant she could let her body run on autopilot while she scanned the crowd for signs of her creepy stalker.

Had that woman seriously followed her all the way down to Islamorada? Seriously? Could Rina not escape her for even an entire week? And here she'd thought her little vacation jaunt down to the Keys was just what she needed to escape the morbid reality she had left behind in Naples.

But then, why should she be surprised her headaches had followed her? Wasn't that the way her world worked? No matter how far she ran, no matter how hard she tried, she couldn't quite escape the things she had been avoiding.

As she mingled around the crowd, she couldn't find any sign of Debbie. Nor could she find Beth again. It should have been easy enough to find a single server at a wedding, but apparently not. Had she left instead of changing her outfit? God, had she even worked for the caterer? Or had she just stolen a uniform to get close to her?

It certainly would have explained why she'd been so clumsy.

But, the more she thought about the girl, the more she looked like a female version of Conner in her mind. It had to be her imagination going wild, didn't it? There was no way that girl had looked anything like her son. It just wasn't possible...

Her chest tightened. Rina's head whipped around, her eyes desperately searching for one of the women. She had to get to the bottom of this; she had to put a stop to it one way or another! She couldn't keep running. She couldn't keep hiding. She had to do something about this woman and stop ignoring her.

The chef! Surely he would know all the servers working for him. If she could find him, he could tell her if Beth actually was one of his employees or not. And then...

Rina swirled around, the world spinning along with her. But even when she stopped moving, the world didn't. Rina swayed, trying to get a grip on herself. But even as she struggled to breathe, everything went dark, and her knees gave out.

"Rina!" Steve's voice cut through the fog. Strong hands gripped her and lifted her up out of the sand.

Rina blinked a few times, trying to get the world to stop freaking spinning. What was going on?

"Easy, just take it slow." Steve held her, his voice helping to guide her back to reality. He kept talking in a soothing tone until her vision cleared and she locked eyes with him. Then, he let out a breath and smiled. "Jesus, Rina! Did you eat anything at all today?"

"Not unless you count coffee," a voice said from her right. Holly? Rina thought blearily. Turning her head was like moving through molasses, but when she finally did, the woman speaking certainly looked like her older sister except... didn't. Rina stared at her, struggling to make the pieces to the puzzle fit in place. Then, it clicked. Gabby! It wasn't Holly; it was her daughter.

"I feel like crap," Rina groaned out, making Steve chuckle. She was standing upright again, but Steven kept his hands on her, making sure she didn't go anywhere. Rina forced herself to smile. "Sorry, I don't usually faint at weddings... I've just..."

"Been under a lot of stress?" Steve finished for her, and she nodded. That was probably the understatement of the year, but Steve didn't need to know just how crazy things had gotten.

"I should go back to the house, lay down for a bit." It wasn't exactly what Rina wanted to do, but now that the wedding was winding down, she wasn't needed around there anymore. Thankfully the majority of the guests had already left, along with the bride and groom, so not many people had seen her little episode.

"I'll drive you back. Come on." Rina opened her mouth to protest, but Steve cut her off. "Don't even try it. I owe you for saving my daughter's wedding. The least I can do is drive you back to the house. And that doesn't even scratch the surface of repaying you for making all this happen."

Rina nodded and let him guide her toward the edge of the beach. She would argue with him later. She just didn't have the strength to do it right then.

Between the normal stress of making sure a wedding went off without a hitch and then adding Beth showing up on top of it, Rina was mentally and physically exhausted.

When the Inn came into view, towering over the open grass that surrounded it, and with the beach and cabins off in the distance, Rina let out a sigh. One of the longest days of her life was almost over. They just had to drive a little bit further to the house itself, then Rina could crawl upstairs and collapse into her bed.

Her problems would still be there in the morning, she decided, and she could face them then.

But when Steve pulled up in front of the Archer House, her heart stopped. Sitting on the old wooden swing on the beach were the two women Rina wanted to see least in her life. And that was up until a week ago; her sisters would have been at the top of that list.

Rina let out a sigh as she unfastened her seatbelt. The universe wasn't going to let her avoid this one, it seemed. It was time for her to face them, whether she wanted to or not.

CHAPTER TWENTY-ONE

Steve, ever the gentleman, helped her out of the car. She wanted to invite him inside, offer him a cup of coffee or something, but she couldn't. At least this time, she had an excuse for running off on him.

"Thank you for the ride home. I really appreciate it." To her surprise, she actually stepped forward and hugged the man. He hugged her back, and she had to fight to keep from melting against him. God, she wanted to just give in to her instincts and welcome him back into her life, but she couldn't. "I've got some friends I need to catch up with."

Steve followed her gaze toward the two women sitting on the swing. "You sure you're okay? Don't want me to stay with you?"

God, did she ever want him to stay with her. But she knew that wouldn't be a great idea. This was something she had to handle herself alone. She wasn't going to drag Steve into her family drama. She was sure he had enough on his own plate to worry about.

"I'll be fine," she assured him with a nod, smiling at him. She still wanted to crawl into bed and sleep for about a week, but at least she didn't feel like passing out anymore. That had to count for something, right?

Steve studied her for a moment, making her shiver under the intense scrutiny. Then, he finally nodded, breaking the hug and stepped back toward the car. Rina stood rooted in place, watching him drive off, every moment wanting to yell for him to come back.

Then she looked over at Gabby and gave her the same smile. "Go on inside and see how your mother's doing. I'll be in in a little while."

Gabby didn't look any more pleased about being dismissed than Steve did. But just like him, she didn't argue. Rina figured both Gabby and Holly would be watching her from inside, but she decided she didn't much care. As long as they were inside and not sneaking around eavesdropping, she could deal with having someone keep an eye on her—especially if she fainted again.

Once Gabby was inside, Rina took a deep breath and held it. She braced herself for the upcoming confrontation, steeling herself to get it over with. She wanted to be done with Debbie and her lies wanted to move on with her life instead of living in the past and listening to her unfounded stories.

Rina's body moved on its own. Her hands balled into fists at her sides, nails biting into the tender flesh of her palm. Even the fresh sea air that wafted over on the gentle breeze wasn't enough to quell the anger that had welled up inside her.

"You've got a lot of nerve, following me out here like this. What the hell were you thinking?" Rina demanded. She couldn't ever remember being so angry. No, scratch that. She had been that angry once before in her life when she'd finally broken things off with Steve all those years ago.

Debbie stood from the swing and turned to face Rina. She didn't speak; she just looked into Rina's eyes as she reached into her purse. Moments later, she pulled out what looked like a photo, then handed it to Rina. "Believe me now?"

Rina stared at the photograph she'd just been handed. That was Dennis, all right, though he was much younger than the last time she had seen him. He grinned at the camera; a small newborn baby swaddled in his arms. But Rina had seen all the photographs of him and Conner and Trevor after they had been born. This most certainly wasn't one of them.

She looked up at Beth, squinting. She could see the resemblance to Conner again, and her heart raced. She thought back to the conversation she'd had with Debbie that night at the bar before things had gone south. "You're seventeen?"

Beth bit her bottom lip and then nodded.

She thought back, seventeen years ago. Conner would have been one, and Trevor would've been four. That was the same time Rina had been working on building her business in Naples, trying to become established in a competitive market and raise two rambunctious boys at the same time.

What had Dennis been doing? That was a silly question for her to have asked. Dennis had been doing the same thing he had always been doing - working. He'd always told her he was too busy to help take care of the kids. Getting a nanny to watch them during the days had been his brilliant solution.

But it had been more than that, hadn't it? He hadn't been working late nights, toiling away in the office. He'd been out with

Debbie, messing around. How could she have been so stupid? How could she have not noticed the signs that he had been cheating on her?

God, she was so, so stupid.

She let out a long string of curses. She so badly wanted to tear the photo up, wanted to crumble it into a ball, and then toss it out into the sea. She wanted to keep her head buried in the sand, to pretend her marriage had always been perfect, that they'd always been happy together and taken care of each other.

"I'm sorry," Rina said at last. Her anger had faded into numbness. She passed the photo back to Debbie; her mind was still reeling with this new information. "I never knew. All these years and I never knew. I'm such an idiot."

Rina broke after that. Tears formed at the corners of her eyes, and nothing she did could stop them from spilling onto her cheeks. No matter how many times she wiped them away, they just kept coming. Her entire body shook as she started sobbing. After all the stress of the day, all the stress of the last six months, she just couldn't take it anymore. She couldn't keep it all bottled up inside her any longer.

The next thing she knew, arms had wrapped around her, pulling her into a hug. She thought it was Steve at first, having come back to save her once again. But the arms were smaller, thinner. And while they held her tight, they didn't have the same strength as Steve's. Then, she thought it had to have been Debbie or Beth, having felt sorry for the poor woman who'd just had her life turned upside down.

But when she forced her eyes open, blinking away the tears long enough to see clearly, it wasn't either of them holding her. It was Holly. She looked at Rina with concern in her eyes, and Rina had no doubt she'd been right in her assumption that Holly had been watching at the window. But she had never expected her older sister to swoop in and comfort her like that.

"Are you going to be okay?" Holly asked, her voice low and soft. She looked deep into Rina's eyes, searching for something in her gaze.

Rina had to force herself to nod. She most certainly didn't feel okay. But she knew, eventually, she would be able to get herself under control again. It was just going to take time, time to figure everything out and wrap her head around it all.

Holly returned the nod and then looked over at the two women still standing there awkwardly. "Do you guys need a place to stay for the night?" Holly asked.

"Actually..." Debbie took a deep breath and then let it out slowly. "We do."

CHAPTER TWENTY-TWO

HOLLY GUIDED RINA OVER TO THE SWING, AND SHE COLLAPSED onto it; still, shell shocked from learning her husband wasn't the man she had thought he was. In her eyes, he had always been such a perfect husband. Well, at least Rina had thought he'd been perfect. She had always just thought he'd been working hard to support his family. She never once thought he would ever cheat on her. He'd never had a reason to, she had thought.

Holly left her there with her thoughts for a little while, taking Debbie and Beth over to the Inn to get them settled for the night. Debbie handed Rina the photo back, and for the longest time, Rina just sat there and stared at it. She didn't want to believe her husband would cheat on her. Why would he? Rina had always been good to him. She'd worked to build her business so she wouldn't just be leaching off him. She had taken care of their children and made sure the house was always in order. She'd always tried not to nag him about the long hours he had worked.

So why would he ever cheat on her?

It just didn't make sense.

And yet, Rina couldn't argue with the photo in her hands. She couldn't argue with how much that girl looked like her son. No matter how badly she wanted to bury her head in the sand and pretend everything was just some elaborate scheme, there was only so long she could hide from the truth.

"How're you holding up?" Holly's sudden voice made Rina jump. She looked up to see Holly standing right in front of her, a sad smile on her face.

Rina sighed, then shrugged. How was she holding up? Barely at all seemed to be the appropriate response, but she also couldn't bring herself to say the words out loud. She shook her head as her heart pounded hard in her chest. It felt like it would break free at any moment.

But Holly seemed to understand. She nodded, then sat down next to her and held her hand out for the photo. Rina passed it over, glad to have it out of her sight for at least a few moments.

God, how was she going to tell the boys about this? It was going to absolutely ruin the image of their father. While she had no doubt they'd both welcome Beth into the family with open arms, she couldn't bring herself to trample over their memories.

"What do I do?" Rina found herself asking aloud, less to Holly and more to herself. She would have to tell the boys at some point, though she had no idea how.

Holly shrugged, setting the photo down on her lap. "I wish I had the answer for you, I really do. But there are no easy answers to something like this. It's... it's hard to move forward after finding out your husband wasn't the man you thought he was, you know? But at least now, you know. Now you can start figuring out how you can move forward, even if it's just an inch at a time."

"What if I don't want to move forward?" Rina asked in only a whisper. Eventually, she would have to, but dang if she didn't feel ready for that yet. She was still just coming to terms with Dennis's death, and now she had to deal with finding out he had cheated on her? And God, if he'd cheated on her once, how many other times might he have done it? How many other kids might he have running around out there?

Holly smiled and bumped her shoulder against Rina's. For the first time since they were kids, Rina actually felt like she and her sister were on the same team. God, she hadn't realized just how much she missed that. "I doubt life really cares what you want. It certainly didn't care what I wanted."

"You know, I actually came out here, trying to get away from Debbie and the accusations." When Holly looked at her with a raised eyebrow, she explained about her encounter with Debbie at the bar.

"Yeah, I don't blame you. I would have assumed she was a money grabber too. I guess I should feel lucky. My husband was stealing from everyone and cheating on me, but at least he never knocked anyone up that I know of!"

"I'll remind you of that when a whole brood of kids come forward," Rina teased. Then, she let out a sigh and shook her head. "I guess I do kind of owe her a part of what Dennis left behind, don't I? I mean, she is his kid and that entitles her to something. At the very least, I should make sure she has enough for college. Dennis had made sure the boys had enough for it, so I should do the same for her."

"You're a good person, you know that? Not many people would be willing to give money to their husband's illegitimate child. Though, I guess if she really wanted to push it, she could contest the will for a share of. Though I'm not sure if she can do that six months after the fact."

Rina smiled to herself and wiped the tears off her cheeks as Holly started to babble. Honestly, she had no idea what Beth would have been legally entitled to. But legally or not, she knew she owed the girl something. She'd grown up without her father, and now that he was gone, shouldn't she get something out of that?

"And hey, even if you did come home just to run away from a crazy woman, I know Mom's thrilled to have you back here. She's been in even higher spirits than before. I think the party tomorrow is going to be good for her."

"What about Amy?" Rina asked, wondering about their youngest sister. Tomorrow they'd have three of the four kids together for the first time in ages. Rina could only imagine how excited their mother would be if all four of them had managed to get together again.

Holly shook her head, gazing wistfully out at the water. The beautiful pinks and reds and oranges were back as the sun dipped below the horizon. Soon, they would be in the dark, but neither of them was in any rush to head inside. "I've called and texted her a couple of times, but she hasn't responded. Randy said he hasn't heard from her either. So I guess it's just going to be the three of us."

"I hope she's okay," Rina said. Her lips curved down into a frown, her brow furrowed. It had been too long since she'd seen her little sister. And though they hadn't exactly been best friends when they were younger, she hadn't felt the same animosity toward her as she had with Holly. They were just different people and drifted apart. And all that was in the past now. "I'll try giving her a call. Maybe she'll answer for me. Then again, if she's not even talking to Randy, I guess I shouldn't get my hopes up."

"Maybe after the party, we should all drive out there and check on her. I guess we might just end up with the door slammed in our face, but it's gotta be worth a shot, right?"

Rina nodded. That sounded like a solid plan to her. Even if they did end up getting turned away at the door, they could at least say they had tried. Not doing anything other than calling or texting just didn't seem right.

But, at the same time, there was only so much they could do.

CHAPTER TWENTY-THREE

Rina sighed, staring at the door in front of her, eyes tracking each scratch and scuff mark. She had seen that door a thousand times, just like every room in the Inn. She had been in and out of each of them more times than she could count. And yet, she'd never been this nervous before.

She raised her hand to knock, then froze. Why was this so danged hard? Why couldn't she just talk to them and get it over with? Hadn't she decided last night she wasn't going to run from this anymore, that she was going to face it head-on and deal with whatever fallout came from it?

So why did she hesitate? Why couldn't she bring herself to knock?

Shaking her head, she took a deep breath. She was stronger than this. She could do this, dang it. She wasn't going to let two strangers get to her like that.

She knocked three times, the sound seeming to echo down the

hallway. Her heart pounded just as loud, her mouth going dry. God, she was a grown woman and yet there she was, contemplating if she could make it down the hallway and around the corner before they answered the door. She forced herself to stay rooted to the ground, though, refusing to give in to her instincts this time. Sometimes they were right, but this wasn't one of them.

She had to face Debbie and Beth, no matter how much she wanted to do anything else.

When the door opened, Beth stood there. She froze when she saw Rina, staring awkwardly.

"Good morning," Rina forced out, trying her best to smile and look happy to see them. "I wanted to invite you and your mom to breakfast this morning. The Archer Inn has one of the best chefs on the island, and he makes an amazing breakfast with a gorgeous view of the beach."

She had given Randy instructions on how to start setting everything up, making plans to come check on him after breakfast. She couldn't spend all day with Debbie and Beth, but she wanted to talk to them for a little while, at least. There was so much they had to talk about. So much Rina had to come to terms with.

Debbie appeared behind Beth, putting her hands on her daughter's shoulders before nodding. "We'd love to join you. I guess we still have a lot to talk about, don't we?"

Being the daughter of the owner certainly had its perks. Despite the restaurant being quite busy that morning, Rina was able to get them a table outside relatively quickly. As they sipped on glasses of ice-cold water, Rina looked out over the beach and tried to figure out where to even start.

"How long were you and Dennis together?" Rina asked at last.

She kept her gaze on the beach, unable to even look at the woman her husband had cheated on her with. It was all still so raw, and she was barely even able to keep herself from having another breakdown like she had done the night before.

She had this time, though. They were in public now, and Holly wasn't around to come to her rescue. She was on her own.

"About five years. He stuck around until Beth was four, and then decided to break it off." Debbie let out a breath, then took a sip of her water again. "Said it was too risky to keep things going. And here I thought he loved me. He always told me he planned on leaving you for me. So, if it makes you feel any better, you're not the only one he lied to."

Rina nodded. It didn't make her feel better. If anything, it made her feel even worse. Maybe if he really had fallen in love with someone else, she could have come to terms with it back then. Just because she had loved him didn't mean he'd loved her.

But that wasn't the case it seemed. He had cheated on her with another woman, one he'd had no intentions of sticking around for. No doubt, if she hadn't gotten pregnant, he would have broken it off sooner and moved on to someone else.

God, Rina could barely even bring herself to wonder how many other women there had been over the years. He had always been busy working long hours, and now Rina wondered just how many of those were actually spent working and how many had been spent with other women.

Debbie picked up her purse and then pulled out a couple more photos, sliding them across the table. "I wasn't sure, but I thought you might want to see these, too."

Rina nodded, the words stuck in her throat. Even if she'd

wanted to ignore the photo from last night, she couldn't ignore all of them. They showed Beth at various ages, alongside her father. There was no plausible reason why Dennis would have taken all these photos if he wasn't her father.

When she was little, she really did look like Conner except with longer hair. If they'd been raised together, people probably would have thought they were twins. The more she looked at the photos, the more she knew the truth.

Dennis was Beth's father. Dennis had cheated on her. Not just once either, but he'd been with Debbie for at least five years. Five whole years she'd been at home, raising Conner and Trevor while her husband was out and about with another family, living a completely separate life.

Rina slid the photos back across the table. She had always wanted a daughter, but this wasn't how she'd wanted it to happen. Sure, she wasn't technically Beth's mother, wasn't even really her step-mother, but she was something to the girl, right?

"Look, I don't know what you're legally entitled to since Dennis didn't include you in the will, but I'm going to call the lawyer who handled it and talk to him about the best way to proceed. I'm sure he's going to want a paternity test done, just to cover all the bases. Though it's not like anyone can really argue with the photos, but you know how lawyers are. At the very least, I'll make sure you have enough to cover your college expenses."

Beth was quiet, but she nodded. She chewed on her bottom lip, staring at the photos still lying on the table. When she looked up at Rina, there were tears in the corners of her eyes. "I only vaguely remember him from when I was little. Do you think... Would you be able to give me a couple more photos of him from after he left us?"

"Of course," Rina said immediately. She probably had hundreds of them lying around at the house. It wasn't anything to give Beth some of them. Rina would have wanted more photos of her father if she hadn't gotten to know him growing up.

Heck, now that she thought about it, she did want more photos of her father. She would have to sit down with her mom after the party and get copies of some of them. Sure, she'd gotten to spend her entire childhood with both parents happily married, but she had distanced herself from them for most of her adult life.

She could only imagine how many memories she had missed out on. She could've been here with them, helping build the Inn into something bigger and better. She should have been there with her kids, letting them spend more time with their grandparents.

Rina wondered what her life would have been like if she'd returned to Islamorada after college instead of moving to Naples. She could have easily set up an event planning business here way back then. Having the built-in connection to the Archer Inn when it was still in its prime would have given her a leg up back when she'd been struggling to book clients.

Their waiter brought food over after that, and being able to stuff themselves while they talked helped break the ice a little bit. Beth asked about her father, what foods he liked, what hobbies he had enjoyed. Rina answered the questions as best she could, trying not to be bitter about the whole thing.

It was strange, holding a grudge against a dead man. She wished Debbie had come forward sooner. Then she could have at least confronted Dennis and gotten some closure out of everything.

But now... now he was gone, and she would never get to talk to him about everything.

But that wasn't their fault. Sure, she was still a little mad at Debbie for having slept with a married man, but not nearly as angry as she was at Dennis for breaking their marriage vows—for breaking her trust.

She would have to find some way to come to terms with it all, but she wasn't sure how. Once the party was over, she wanted to sit and talk with Holly, find out how she'd dealt with everything. Her situation had been completely different than Rina's, but it was all about broken trust. If there was one person who understood what Rina was going through, it would be Holly.

They were half-way through breakfast when the door leading into the restaurant opened. Rina's breath caught in her throat as she looked at Conner, Trevor, and Shannon, stepping out into the sunlight. She had completely forgotten they'd agreed to come out for their grandmother's party this afternoon.

Silently, Rina cursed herself for being so airheaded. She had so much going on that she was starting to lose her mind.

Rina took a deep breath and then let it out slowly, trying to calm her pounding heart. "My boys are here for my mother's seventieth birthday party this afternoon. Please don't say anything to them yet. I want to be the one to tell them, and I figure it's a conversation better to be had in private, you know?"

Beth and Debbie looked at each other. They seemed to be speaking without even saying a word out loud. Finally, they both nodded in agreement just as Trevor spotted Rina, the three of them making a beeline through the crowded patio.

"Hey, Mom!" Conner said, grinning broadly. "Long time no see. Enjoying your beach vacation?"

"Oh, you know it!" Rina plastered a matching smile on her face as she stood to hug her sons and hopefully soon-to-be daughter-in-law. "I was just having breakfast with an old friend and her daughter. Would you guys like to join us?"

Rina wasn't thrilled about keeping the truth from them, but it was for the best. They could have a family heart-to-heart after Nelly's party. Until then, she wanted to keep things as stress-free as possible so everyone could have a good day.

CHAPTER TWENTY-FOUR

BY THE TIME RINA LED HER GROUP OVER TO WHERE THEY were setting up for the party, Randy had everything set up just the way she and Holly had planned. He laughed when he saw her shocked expression, then winked and nudged her in the ribs.

"See, your little brother can follow directions!" he teased with a laugh.

Rina nodded and then hugged Randy as she thanked him. No matter how much he grew up, it was hard for Rina to see him as anything other than her annoying little brother. But he wasn't the little kid who was always getting into trouble anymore.

"Boo!" a voice yelled from behind her.

Rina jumped and let out a very unladylike squeal as she whirled around to see Steve and Jake burst into laughter. She glared at the two of them as her heart rate slowly returned to its normal speed. Randy may have done a good bit of growing up since they were kids, but apparently, those two hadn't.

But that was fine. If they wanted to act like children, Rina could handle that. She had raised two boys already and knew just how to punish childish behavior. "Well, I'm glad the two of you showed up early. Guess who just volunteered to cart the ladders around and hang up all the banners and streamers Holly picked out?"

Both of them groaned as Rina grinned broadly. She'd planned on doing that part herself, or at the very least volunteering Conner and Trevor to do it, but if these two wanted to act like they were the children, then they could do the tedious parts of decorating.

"Speaking of Holly, where is she?" Jake asked, looking around. No doubt he was hoping his new girlfriend would get him out of his punishment, but he was out of luck this time.

"She's currently out having breakfast with Mom. Then they were going to spend some time strolling through the park. As far as Mom knows, she's going to get to spend a meal with each of us today. She had no idea we've planned a party for her!"

Rina was actually quite proud of how well they had kept everything from their mother. She'd thought for sure Nelly would have figured it out by now, but either her mental health was in worse shape than they thought, or she was just so happy to have three of her four kids back home for once, she wasn't going to question things.

Personally, Rina was hoping for the latter option.

She walked over and stood between the guys, slinging an arm over each of their shoulders. Sure, she had to stand on her toes to do it, but it had the needed effect and they slumped a bit as she guided them to where the boxes of decorations had been set.

"Well, I guess I do owe you," Steve teased as he picked up the sixteen-foot ladder that had been set aside specifically for hanging decorations. "You could not believe how ecstatic Avery was when I dropped them off at the airport this morning. I'm surprised they even needed the plane. She was practically walking on air as it was!"

Rina laughed and nodded. She had seen enough brides after their wedding to know exactly what Steve was talking about. No doubt, her new husband had been just as excited, but men tended to be a bit more controlled with their emotions.

"Where did she decide to go for her honeymoon?" She had meant to ask Avery what her plans were for after the wedding, but she had never gotten around to it. With everything else going on, other things had been more important than discussing honeymoon plans, as fun as they were. If Rina had, had more time working on the wedding, they would have talked about it, but even when the other planner had already set everything in motion, there was still a ton of work to do during the week leading up.

"Maine."

Rina stopped and blinked at Steve. Surely he hadn't just said... But the deadpan look he gave her said he had indeed. Sure, it was summer, but it was the end of summer and Maine wasn't exactly known for being warm even during the best of times. She let out a dramatic sign and shook her head.

"I guess when you live in paradise, it's hard to choose a proper honeymoon destination," Rina teased, making Steve laugh.

"I tried to steer her in a better destination, but... you know how teenage girls are." Steve shrugged, holding his hands up in defeat. "I can't say I've ever understood how their brains worked."

Rina rolled her eyes, knowing that was a subtle jab at her. Sure, she hadn't always been rational as a teenager, but he was the one who couldn't decide which sister he really wanted to hook up with.

"Teenage boys aren't much better. They have a habit of thinking with the wrong head." She gave him a pointed look, and he looked properly chastised, nodding in agreement.

"That they don't..." He glanced over at Jake, who was still frowning at the stack of boxes they were now responsible for. "But I guess we better get to work if we want this place looking good before your mom gets back. How much time do we have?"

Rina checked her watch and then fought back a groan. Her breakfast had taken longer than she had planned since the kids had joined her. "We've got just about three hours before she'll be back here expecting Randy to take her out to lunch. And if everything isn't perfect by then, it's Holly who's going to be out for blood."

Jake perked up at that, his eyes going wide. Then, he stared at the boxes with a renewed sense of horror. Now, not only was putting up the decorations a minor inconvenience but if he didn't get it done in time, his girlfriend was likely to murder him for it.

Everyone knew just how much of a perfectionist Holly was, and delivering less than perfect results was not something even Rina recommended.

"Good luck, boys!" she said with a wink before sauntering off to check with how everything else was going on.

RINA FLITTED AROUND THE PARTY, CHECKING ON EVERYTHING. Holly wasn't the only perfectionist in the family. Even though this party was technically Holly's responsibility, there was no way Rina was letting an event she was involved with be anything less than perfect.

But once again, everyone was pretty well on the ball. She did have to prod Steve and Jake a few times to keep them from slacking off, but it didn't take much more than a sharp look to get Jake scrambling back up the ladder.

Rina almost wished it was Steve climbing instead of being the one to keep the ladder steady and pass the decorations up. As much as she enjoyed the sight of Jake's backside, Holly had already laid her claim on him, and she wasn't going to get in the middle of that.

Besides, she thought with a smirk that Steve's looked better anyway.

Beth and Debbie even volunteered to help, helping set out table clothes and other small decorations. Rina chatted with them as time allowed, the three of them sharing stories about Dennis. It was so strange, telling them about all the happy times she'd had with the man when she'd never been more angrier with him.

Though that wasn't nearly as strange as hearing the stories they told her. It was hard to believe there was so much about the man she had shared her life with that he'd kept from her. She had let herself get so wrapped up in the kids and her job that she hadn't realized he had been lying to her the entire time.

And here she had thought she'd had the perfect marriage, just like her parents.

It really showed just how much she'd had her head buried in the sand.

"Are Dad's parents still alive?" Beth asked at one point. She looked hopeful like there might be another party like this in her future, one for an actual biological grandparent.

Rina hated to squash the girl's hopes, but she shook her head. "No, Dennis's parents died awhile back. I have some pictures of them back at the house, though. I'll make sure you get copies of those too."

It wasn't much, but at least it would give the girl some small connection to her paternal family. Dennis didn't have any siblings either, so other than Conner and Trevor, she had no other relatives from that side of the family.

Rina glanced over at her brother, laughing as he flexed his muscles after setting down a load of chairs. She had despised her family for so long, but now she realized just how lucky she had been, growing up with such a large family.

She really had been blind, but now she was going to make up for all that lost time.

CHAPTER TWENTY-FIVE

Almost back. Send Randy to meet us at the house.

Rina read the text message and then grinned. That meant the secret was still safe, and Nelly had no idea about the party she was about to walk into. Rina rushed over to Randy, showing him the message, and he grinned just as broadly.

Once back at the house, Holly would leave Randy with their mother, then rush over to meet everyone at the party. Randy would talk their mother into going for a nice stroll before heading to lunch, and then everyone who had arrived would surprise her and hopefully not give her a heart attack.

There were about sixty or so people that had already arrived. They were milling around the grounds talking and gossiping. To them, a party was just an excuse to get out of the house and exchange whatever tidbits of gossip they'd collected since the last time they saw each other.

As much as Rina loved being back in Islamorada, that was one part of a small town, she was never going to like. There wasn't a whole lot going on, which left the locals with far more time on their hands than was healthy. And so, they spent all that free time gabbing with each other nonstop.

If she really was going to move back there, she would have to find some way to occupy herself! Because while Rina loved her mother to death, that was not the kind of retirement she was looking forward to.

With any luck, she would be spending her retirement with lots of little grandbabies running around the island. Something her mother hadn't truly gotten to enjoy, all because she'd raised four hard-headed kids.

When Holly came running over, everyone went quiet. Holly bent over, hands resting on her knees as she gasped for air. It took a few moments before she had the strength to look up at everyone and grin, giving them a thumbs up. "She'll be here soon!" Holly announced.

Now everyone was grinning. Everyone kept their voice to whispers, not wanting to spoil the surprise. With any luck, Nelly wouldn't have any idea about the party until she walked right smack into it.

The seconds ticked into minutes, everyone shifting from foot to foot. Rina stared out in the direction of the house, practically holding her breath as she waited for Randy and Nelly to appear. Any moment now, they would crest the small hill that hid the party from view.

Small dots appeared in the distance, inching higher and higher. Rina squinted the grinned as Randy and Nelly came into view. She grinned broader than ever when they both stopped at the top.

Randy braced his mother as she started shaking, staring with an open mouth at the mass of people assembled below.

"Happy Birthday!" everyone shouted. The voices echoed around the Inn, and Rina had no doubt that Nelly had been able to hear them clear as day.

Randy nudged her along, and when she got closer, Rina could see the tears in her mother's eyes. She tried to wipe them away with her sleeve, but they just kept coming. Despite that, she grinned broadly, and it was obvious just how much she appreciated the effort they had made for her.

Holly met them first, wrapping her arms around Nelly and wishing her a happy birthday. Rina was next, hugging her mother tight. Nelly hugged her back, tears smearing across Rina's shirt.

God, she really had missed this.

Once she finally released Rina, the three siblings encouraged their mother to greet the rest of the assembled people. Gabby's fiancé had driven down, as had Holly's son and his girlfriend. Randy had tried to get his daughters to come visit, but his ex-wife was apparently still not taking his calls.

Rina had a few choice words for the woman, but none of them were appropriate for polite company.

She introduced Nelly to Debbie and Beth, though she kept her relationship with them a secret. She still wasn't quite ready to share that information yet, and Rina knew just how well her mother liked to gossip. If anyone other than Holly found out, it would only be a matter of time before someone spilled the beans to her boys, and she really didn't want them finding out that particular secret from the grapevine.

Once Nelly had greeted her assembled family members, Holly

signaled for the kitchen staff to bring out the cakes. When Nelly spotted the line of people carrying confectionery, she started crying again. Rina wasn't even sure if she heard the audience singing Happy Birthday to her.

But it didn't matter, not really. To Nelly, the details just weren't important. She didn't care if the tables were perfectly arranged. She didn't care about the banners and streamers and other decorations that were hung all over the area.

She just cared about the people who had taken the time to come see her. She cared about all the effort they put into making her birthday something special. Even if the party had been a complete dumpster fire, Nelly still would've been thrilled just because everyone had cared enough to try.

Steve walked over a few minutes later, carrying two plates of cake. He grinned as he offered her one and then nodded toward the beach. "Feel like taking a short walk with me?"

"As long as this one doesn't last the entire day," she teased, winking at him.

Steve laughed, and the two of them headed in the direction of the crashing waves. Rina savored the cake, letting the sweetness wash over her tongue. It probably had a month's worth of sugar in it, but she didn't care. It was simply divine even if she did feel herself gaining weight with each bite. Not to mention inching closer and closer to diabetes.

"The party seems like a raging success. I don't think I've ever seen your mother that happy. She looks almost as happy as Avery was this morning!"

"Guess that means all the long hours were worth it! I just wish Amy had been able to make it. I know Mom is just happy having three of us home for her birthday, but I was really hoping she would come out for it." Rina smiled sadly at her last bite of cake. She wasn't sure what was going on with her younger sister, but she was going to find out. Or, at the very least, she was going to try. "Holly and I are going to drive out and see her sometime this week. Check-in and make sure she's okay, you know?"

Steve nodded. He smiled, the nudged her with his shoulder and winked. "I'm sure she's just fine. You Archer women are pretty tough cookies. But it's good you're going out to see her. It's never too late to start fresh, is it?"

"No, maybe it's not."

Steve turned to face her. He stood only inches away, his eyes locked onto hers. Rina couldn't even breathe. She was trapped there, locked in some kind of trance. Steve smiled, and a shiver went through her body. She'd been talking about starting over with Amy moments ago, but deep down, Steve was the one she really wanted a second chance with.

"There's something I didn't get a chance to do yesterday..." His voice was barely above a whisper. Even though there wasn't anyone around to overhear him, Rina could tell his words were meant only for her.

When she raised an eyebrow, Steve smiled even broader. Then, he leaned down and pressed his lips to hers. Electricity surged through her body. Every nerve stood on end as Rina leaned into the kiss, kissing him right back.

She was breathless in only moments. Tears stung at the corners of her eyes, and she quickly wiped them away. "That woman? Debbie? She was Dennis's mistress. Beth is their daughter." The words came out in a rush. Rina forced herself to keep going, knowing if she stopped, she wouldn't be able to start again. "God, only a couple days back in Islamorada and my whole life's been turned upside down. I mean, things are going better with Holly and Randy than they have in years, but I just found out my dead husband had been cheating on me for God only knows how long. And I still have to tell the boys, but I don't know how I can possibly do that without crushing their memory of him."

Steve blinked at her, taking in everything she had said. He nodded, looking at her with compassion in his eyes. His marriage with Jennifer may not have been comparable to Rina's, but he understood what it was like to be lost and confused.

"I guess my point is, I've got a lot of baggage with me this time. But... if that doesn't bother you, then I would like to give this another shot. See how it works out now that we're both adults."

Steve reached up and cupped her cheek, wiping away a stray tear with his thumb. He smiled at her, and she didn't see even an ounce of indecision or fear in his eyes. "Seeing Avery get married yesterday changed a lot of things for me. My life has been a mess ever since I'd married Jennifer. But seeing her up on that altar, seeing how happy she was, it made me realize there are still good things in this world. And that sometimes, those good things are worth all the hassle that comes with them."

Before Rina could say anything, Steve leaned forward and kissed her again, sending more fireworks dancing through her body. She giggled, grinning up at him. "I take it that's a yes then?"

"Well, if you have to ask, I must really be out of practice." Steve winked at her, and Rina burst out laughing.

Maybe this time, things would work out between them. They'd both grown up a lot since their high school days and learned a lot.

And running away from her past hadn't worked so well before, so maybe it was time to face things head-on. She couldn't run from Islamorada and her family anymore. Nor could she keep running from Debbie and Beth.

But with Steve by her side, just maybe she could find the strength to face it all without falling apart.

You can now Pre – Order Amy's Story
Book Three – When The Stars Align

Other Books by Kimberly

The Archer Inn Series

The Archer House

Winds of Change

www.ingramcontent.com/pod-product-compliance
Lightning Source LLC
LaVergne TN
LVHW092052070325
805404LV00001B/191